It's Homecoming Weekend in Jasper Gulch. Please Join Us As We Salute the Descendants of Our Town's Founding Fathers!

It's been generations since a Massey has set foot in Jasper Gulch, Montana, and the whole town is abuzz over the arrival of Dale Massey, great-great-grandson of one of the town's founders. One hundred years later and people are still talking about the feud that caused a rift between the Masseys and the Shaws.

But now they are also talking about a possible *connection* between a Massey and a Shaw: Dale Massey and Faith Shaw, to be precise. What would a millionaire real estate broker want with the sweet small-town violinist? Has history come full circle? Or will Dale leave town when the photo ops are done, leaving Faith and her loving heart behind?

* * *

Big Sky Centennial:
A small town rich in history…and love.

Her Montana Cowboy by Valerie Hansen—*July 2014*
His Montana Sweetheart by Ruth Logan Herne—*August 2014*
Her Montana Twins by Carolyne Aarsen—*September 2014*
His Montana Bride by Brenda Minton—*October 2014*
His Montana Homecoming by Jenna Mindel—*November 2014*
Her Montana Christmas by Arlene James—*December 2014*

Books by Jenna Mindel

Love Inspired

Mending Fences
Season of Dreams
Courting Hope
Season of Redemption
The Deputy's New Family
His Montana Homecoming

JENNA MINDEL

lives in northwest Michigan with her husband and their three dogs. She enjoys a career in banking that has spanned twenty-five years and several positions, but writing is her passion. A 2006 Romance Writers of America RITA® Award finalist, Jenna has answered her heart's call to write inspirational romances set near the Great Lakes.

His Montana
Homecoming

Jenna Mindel

Special thanks and acknowledgment to Jenna Mindel for her contribution to the Big Sky Centennial miniseries.

Recycling programs
for this product may
not exist in your area.

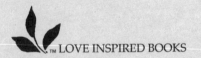

™ LOVE INSPIRED BOOKS

ISBN-13: 978-0-373-81798-6

His Montana Homecoming

Copyright © 2014 by Harlequin Books S.A.

www.Harlequin.com

Printed in U.S.A.

I am with you and will watch over you wherever you go, and I will bring you back to this land. I will not leave you until I have done what I have promised you.
—*Genesis* 28:15

To my fellow authors Valerie Hansen,
Ruth Logan Herne, Carolyne Aarsen, Brenda Minton
and Arlene James—thank you for your insight, your
wealth of knowledge, your patience, but most of all
your friendship. It has been a pleasure!

To Sherry Linnerooth, Executive Director
of the Bozeman Symphony, thank you for
taking the time to answer my many questions.
Your insight is greatly appreciated.

To Rob, thank you for all the interesting little details
like candles in the car and talc mines.

Chapter One

Dale Massey yawned. He was used to traveling, even overseas, but today's flight to Bozeman, Montana, had wiped him out. During the layover in Denver, he'd managed to get some work done but not nearly enough to satisfy him.

Grabbing his suitcase in baggage claim, Dale headed for the rental-car counter. It didn't take long. The airport was small. Wood-beamed ceilings were a novel touch as well as the stonework and robust-patterned carpet. He'd heard that Montana was rugged land, but he'd take Fifth Avenue any day.

In New York, he knew what to expect. And no one expected him to care. He hadn't earned the nickname Dale the Coldheart by shying away from the hard calls in business. His ability to cut through the frills was the reason his father made him in charge of delivering the uncomfortable decisions made by Massey International.

Ten minutes later, Dale kept his voice low and controlled. No need to ever rant. Dale always got what he wanted. "Check again. I have a BMW reserved."

"I'm sorry, but we have no record of that, sir." The young woman's face grew red.

With embarrassment or fear, Dale wasn't sure. He knew his assistant, and Jeannie never let him down. Reserving the 528 Bimmer was a given. The mistake had to be on the rental service, one of only two in the airport.

"Then what do you have available?"

Now the girl looked scared. "An economy car, sir. We're waiting for more vehicles to arrive, just like the other car rental store."

He'd fare no better with their competitor, then. Shaking his head, he signed the paperwork. "How do you run out of cars?"

"It's a big week at the ski resorts and there's this homecoming in Jasper Gulch—"

"I get it." Dale held up his hand to stop the service clerk's overly chipper-sounding rattle.

The girl did her job.

It wasn't her fault that Dale had to represent the Massey family in Jasper Gulch. In an economy rental, no less.

She gave him the keys with trembling fingers. "Right through those double doors. You can't miss the car. It's yellow but it has a turbo engine, no extra charge."

"Thank you."

Shifting his briefcase, Dale found the ugly little car bearing the same color as a lemon. The stupid thing wasn't much bigger than a lemon, either.

He looked around the empty lot. Not much he could do. Only a few more of the nonturbo *toy* cars sat parked. Not even a minivan graced the spaces reserved for rentals. He'd rather be dead than caught in a minivan, but that'd be more comfortable than the *subcompact* before him. Turbo or not.

"Nice." Gritting his teeth, Dale threw his baggage in the rear hatch and then folded his six-foot-two frame into the driver's seat.

He had an hour's drive yet to reach Jasper Gulch. He touched the GPS app on his phone. Jeannie had reserved him a room at the town's one and only inn and downloaded the directions. He started the car and pulled out with a squeal of tires. He aimed to find out how fast this little turbo could go.

By the time Dale drove past the Jasper Gulch, Montana, Welcomes You sign on the one road into town, his spirits had recovered. He had to own that the view of snow-tipped mountains beyond the tiny town impressed him. There was a wide main street with diagonal parking on either side. Dale might as well have stepped back in time. Old pickup trucks and even a couple of *horses* stood *parked* by storefronts that looked straight out of an old Clint Eastwood Western.

Where on earth was he?

He found the hotel he'd been booked into and that's when his good time ended. Leaning against the counter of the Fidler Inn, Dale tried to keep his voice even. "What do you mean my lodging has been changed?"

A gray-haired woman named Mamie Fidler, who owned the place, tapped her foot. "The mayor saw to it personally and has a room for you at Shaw Ranch."

Dale scanned the hokey inn with its crackling fire and various aged people milling around near the warmth. Mamie wore hiking boots with tall woolen socks and a denim skirt. He ran his hand through his hair. He was a long way from Fifth Avenue.

"Well, Mr. Massey? We're full up." Mamie was running out of patience.

So was he. Nothing about this trip had gone as planned. Who changed a person's reservation without asking? And what kind of lodging would he find at this Shaw Ranch—some kind of dude ranch?

He looked at Mamie and sighed. "How do I get there?"

She smiled and pushed a Jasper Gulch Chamber of Commerce illustrated map at him and drew a black marker line to where he needed to go. "See here. Not too far."

Minutes later, Dale was back in the tiny car

headed down a street that bore his last name. He turned north onto Shaw Boulevard and chuckled. Was this place for real? The Masseys had taken off for New York long ago, but the Shaws had stayed and grabbed a grand-sounding name for their street.

The town had been founded by his great-great-grandfather, Silas Massey, along with a man named Ezra Shaw. Dale knew that from what his father, Julian, had told him and from what he'd been able to dig up on internet sites specializing in genealogies. Julian owed him big time for this one.

The road ended outside town at an expanse of green lawn leading to a lavish-looking ranch. Dale followed the winding driveway to the front door under a log archway covered by a large metal roof. Okay, this was more like it. At least they had valet parking. Dale would have to thank the mayor for making the change first chance he got.

He unfolded his legs and stretched. Dale wanted a shower, dinner and sleep, not necessarily in that order. The November sun had set behind the distant mountains, casting a rosy haze across the valley. Talk about a wide-open space. Staring out at the vast land untouched by concrete or steel made him feel small and unworthy.

Dale knew those feelings well. He'd battled them since he was six years old when his father had walked out on him and his mother. But this landscape whispered a challenge, a call to adventure. A man could face himself out here and come up empty or victorious. Which would he be?

Dale shook his head. He wasn't here to face who he was or wasn't. He was here to represent the Massey name.

He opened one of the heavy wooden doors that was pretty hefty for a bed-and-breakfast. Didn't they realize older folks might have trouble with such a door? Not wise for a commercial venture. Didn't they have ordinances in Montana?

He stepped inside. There had to be a valet somewhere.

"Can I help you?"

"Ah, yes…" Dale whirled around at the feminine voice.

A small woman, young, dressed in jeans and a Western-style plaid shirt over a white tank top, cocked her head. Her hair was that reddish-brown color that was neither light nor dark but lush. Her eyes were huge and blue like a storybook princess he'd seen on a preview for a Disney movie.

Those pretty eyes widened as she took in his height. They also looked interested.

"Sort of casual for a valet, don't you think?" He gave her a thorough once-over before tossing her his two keys. "My car's outside."

The keys slapped on the floor.

"Excuse me?" She raised one perfectly arched eyebrow.

Not a valet, then. "Are you the maid?"

The clothes she wore should have been a dead giveaway. Rugged Montana maids wouldn't wear aprons or cleaning uniforms. Of course they'd dress in jeans. And this one looked amazing in them.

Her hands made small fists on her narrow hips. Her head might reach his shoulders if they stood close. "Who are you?"

"Dale Massey."

The lovely girl rolled her eyes as recognition dawned. "I should have known."

Yeah, she should have. Most everyone did. He'd been on the cover of *Fortune* magazine a couple of months ago. But then, not a lot of workers in the service industry read that particular magazine. Maybe this one did.

Dale puffed up his chest in anticipation of the sweet apology she'd deliver. He wouldn't mind seeing those dusty freckles on her nose and cheeks blush a little.

"I guess I'll show you to your room." She didn't sound too thrilled. Not exactly good customer service.

"Don't I have to sign something? Get some keys?"

She pointed to the tiled slate floor. "Your keys are right there and you'll have to move your car. Dad will have a fit if you block the front."

Dale swallowed hard. "Dad?"

She tilted her head. "Mayor Jackson Shaw is my father. I'm Faith Shaw."

"And this place is…" His throat went dry as the air outside.

"Shaw Ranch." A mischievous twinkle shone in her expressive eyes. She enjoyed his discomfort. "Welcome to our home."

So *this* was the infamous Dale Massey who'd been too busy to return her brother Cord's calls. The Centennial Planning Committee had tried for months to get a hold of the Massey family. Cord said they'd been abrupt, dismissive and downright rude at times.

But my, my, my. This man was certainly handsome—in a manicured sort of way. Even the stubble along his jawline looked meticulously groomed. His sleek gray slacks and pristine white shirt with coordinating tie screamed high-end quality. The long tan woolen coat that probably cost a fortune made his green eyes look golden. This man knew exactly how good he looked, too. The smirk on his face confirmed his expectation of fawning adoration.

Faith nearly laughed. He'd get none of that from her. "You want to see the room first or move your car?"

The corner of his shapely mouth twitched. "Move the car. We wouldn't want to anger your father, now, would we?"

She waited for him to pick up his keys. She might be closer, but *he* threw them there.

A slow smile spread across his face. As if they shared a secret.

Faith's belly dropped and her pulse picked up speed. Oh, no. That smile meant big trouble. *He* was trouble. And Faith had a definite weakness for troublesome men.

Dale scooped up his keys with nimble grace and gestured for her to lead the way. "Ladies first."

Now she was a lady? Not the maid or valet?

Faith knew his type well. He had everything but gave nothing. *She* meant nothing to someone like him other than a passing flirtation. Dale Massey struck her as a maestro when it came to the art of male-female relations, and way too rich for her blood in more ways than mere money.

Faith waited for him to catch up and walked alongside him out the double doors. She openly stared at the tiny car in front of her. "You came in that thing?"

"My reservation was lost." He popped the hatch with a click of his key. "Speaking of reservations, why'd your father take it upon himself to move me out here when I was already booked into the Fidler Inn?"

"He thought you'd be more comfortable. The inn's pretty packed with homecoming and all."

Yeah, right!

Faith knew her father's matchmaking when she

smelled it, and Mr. Fancy Pants sure smelled good. Not too much scent, but enough to make a woman want to step closer.

Even though her little sister, Julie, was happily married to a cowboy and her older brother Cord also recently got hitched, Jackson Shaw pushed Faith toward the altar, as well. If it wasn't that anxious banker Wilbur Thompson, it was their pastor who her father encouraged her to chase. They were both good, dependable and solid men. The trouble was, Faith Shaw had never wanted good and dependable. She loved the challenge of a chase. But she'd learned a thing or two when she'd left home. Some wild things didn't want to be tamed.

Faith didn't chase anymore. Not after catching way more than she'd bargained for with Scott in Seattle. Bad boys didn't reform, and flashy flirts were a heartbreak waiting in the wings.

She gave Dale Massey a quick once-over and sighed. He looked like all those things and more. He lifted his designer luggage out of the trunk. No matter how attractive the wrapping, Faith wasn't ready for marriage. If she were, good and dependable would have more appeal. Anyway, she liked her life nice and simple. Dale Massey had complication written all over him.

"Where should I park?"

Faith gathered her wits and pointed. "Around

the corner. Next to my car is fine. It's the navy blue Honda."

Dale nodded and climbed into his rental. Even with the seat pushed back, he looked cramped.

Good! Might knock him down a peg.

Faith gave herself a mental shake. It wasn't nice to wish discomfort on a person. Not exactly her best what-would-Jesus-do moment. She rubbed her arms at the chill in the air and waited for Dale Massey's return.

In moments, he stood tall before her. Very tall. And broad shouldered. Still flashy, though. "Thank you."

"For what?"

Again with the lady-killer smile. "You could have gone inside."

Faith shrugged. Was he being polite or flirting? It shouldn't matter, but tell that to the shiver that raced up her spine. "Come on."

Dale silently followed, but his presence spoke louder than any cymbal. He had a very manly presence for a well-groomed city slicker. She had a feeling this man knew more about high fashion than she did.

Faith spotted her mom charging down the hallway. Ranger, their white poodle, pranced right alongside her.

Faith stopped.

Dale bumped into her. "Sorry."

Faith ignored her skin's gooseflesh at the brief contact. "Mom, this is Dale Massey. Daddy arranged for him to stay here."

Her mother's smile broadened and she extended her hands. "Dale. How good of you to come."

"Mrs. Shaw." He reached for her mother's hand, but Nadine Shaw pulled him into a hearty embrace and even slapped his back before letting go.

Faith bit her lip to keep from laughing at the shock on Dale Massey's face.

"Call me Nadine. Everyone does." Her mom scooped up the dog. "This is Ranger. And it's a pleasure to finally meet you."

"I'm honored." He flashed that smile and ignored the dog.

Nadine pinched his arm, getting mostly wool coat. "Ooohhhh, nice material. Faith, look out for this one. Pastor Ethan's got competition here."

Faith felt her eyes bulge as she gave her mom a pointed look.

But her mother kept going. "Faith's our only daughter left unwed. Julie, our youngest, hitched up last month. As did my oldest boy."

"Mom!"

"Well…it's true." Nadine smiled.

Dale listened with forced interest. This guy was polished with a capital *P,* but he humored her mother, who made them sound like a bunch of backward clodhoppers.

"Show Dale to his room, honey. Your father's at a meeting in town, so dinner will be a late. Dale, you're dining with us." Her mom gave him a wink. "Do you have any allergies we should know about?"

Dale cocked an eyebrow. "None, Nadine. And dinner sounds fine."

If he was put out by her mom's orders, Dale didn't show it. Well, maybe not too visibly, but Faith had seen his chin lift a tad. The man had manners and ironclad control on his facial expressions.

She gestured for him to follow. "Come on."

Dale hoisted his suitcase and followed her without a word. He was probably shell-shocked.

Taking each step of the wide staircase, Faith was aware of every movement made with Dale behind her. What was he thinking? Wait, she didn't want to know. Men like him thought women were trophies or belt-buckle notches.

Not this woman. Faith rubbed her hands, made rough from ranch chores, her fingertips callused from her violin. She was smarter now.

She glanced back at the man who'd be underfoot for at least a week. He'd be around long enough for the homecoming celebration this weekend and the Thanksgiving parade the following week. "Will your family join you?"

A muscle rippled along Dale's jaw. "No."

"Oh." Faith kept moving. They were worlds apart. She couldn't imagine a holiday without family. Maybe she was as naive as ever to think family mattered to everyone.

Cord had told her that Dale was the head of an international real estate services company, built strong by the Massey family. No doubt Dale had been surrounded by important people all his life. She peeked back at him. Right now, he looked terribly alone.

Dale heard the knock at the door but didn't dare move. He had a good spot by the window with a view of the mountains. "It's open."

He'd left the door to his spacious guest room ajar, and Faith slipped inside.

He held up his hand. He'd be with her in a moment. "No, no, no. If they wait on this one, it'll be gone." Then nothing. Silence. "Dad? You there?"

Dale lowered his phone with a growl. "What is it with your cell service? That's the fourth time my call's been dropped."

Faith shrugged her pretty shoulders as if it wasn't a big deal. "We've always had bad coverage here, but we have a landline you can use."

Dale clenched his jaw. He couldn't conduct sensitive business in someone's living room. "Thanks, I'll see how I fare with my laptop."

"Got a piece of paper?"

He handed her his legal pad.

"Here's the password for our internet connection. It's probably slower than what you're used to."

Where was he, the edge of the planet?

He stared at her.

She kept talking, completely unfazed. "If you need privacy, you can use my father's office. It's right before the dining room. Just close the door. He won't mind."

"Thank you." He waited a moment for her to keep chattering.

She didn't. She stared at him, her eyes wide.

"Did you need something?"

"Oh." Her cheeks colored. "Dinner's ready."

She'd changed her clothes. She still wore jeans, but her top was soft and pretty. A gray fuzzy sweater that made her blue eyes glacial. Icy-blue.

He looked down at his rumpled white shirt, which was unbuttoned. He'd been in the process of changing before he'd gotten a call on his cell. No time to shower, but he could wash up and throw on clean clothes. "I'll be a minute."

Her cheeks blazed and she looked anywhere but at him. She backed up and bumped into a chair. "Of course."

He cocked his head, and then it dawned on him that she was embarrassed by his open shirt. His chest wasn't bare; he wore an undershirt. Sure, it fit like a second skin, and maybe that's what had flustered Miss Shaw.

He felt the corners of his mouth twitch.

"You can't miss our dining room. Just follow the noise." She gave him a shy smile and bolted.

Dale stared at the door a moment. Was she for real? Then his phone buzzed and vibrated. "Dale Massey..."

Nothing.

Gritting his teeth, he tossed the phone on the bed and headed for the bathroom to wash up before dinner.

Seriously. Where on earth was he? And how soon could he get done what he came here to do and return to the real world?

Chapter Two

Minutes later, Dale *followed the noise*. Sounds of raucous laughter were hard to miss. He halted at the entrance of the dining room and took in the sight of a long wooden table filled with covered dishes leaking steam. A boisterous family sat at the table. All of them talked at once as they passed pitchers of what looked like pretty tame liquid refreshment. Iced tea and lemonade.

Definitely a rowdier bunch than at the Massey dinner table. But then, the Masseys had never been a real family.

A sudden desire for the overcrowded Fidler Inn swamped him. There, he could have come and gone unnoticed. Downtown Jasper Gulch probably had Wi-Fi, too.

"Dale, there's a seat for you next to Faith." Nadine Shaw smiled. She wasn't obvious. Not at all. "And this is my husband, Mayor Jackson Shaw."

The mayor.

Dale stepped forward and extended his hand. "Mayor Shaw."

The man puffed up his chest as he stood. Brown hair grayed near his temples and held a crease that circled the mayor's head. Dale spotted a black cowboy hat hanging beside others on a hat rack attached to the far wall. No doubt the reason for the crease. Above average height, Jackson Shaw had broad shoulders and he exuded an air of authority. He was also looking Dale over pretty good.

Dale resisted the urge to ask if he liked what he saw.

Finally the mayor gripped his hand for a firm handshake. "Mr. Massey. Good of you to join us."

Dale detected a note of sarcasm in the mayor's voice and swallowed his irritation. He had a life, one he'd dropped in order to be here. "Thank you."

"Let me introduce you to my family. You've met Faith here." Jackson made the rounds.

There was Cord Shaw and his new wife, Katie, and their goddaughter, Marci, whom they were planning to adopt. Cord's brothers, Austin and Adam, and then the youngest sibling, Julie, and her husband, Ryan. Dale sat down, knowing he'd have trouble remembering the names. Didn't matter. He'd stay through the weekend and leave. He'd be here only a few days at most.

"Let's pray, shall we?" The mayor cleared his

throat and shifted his stance as he took the hands of his wife and youngest daughter seated on either side of him.

Everyone else followed suit. Faith offered up her hand and so did her brother—Austin, was it?

Okay, this is weird. He took Faith's hand easily enough, but then Dale hesitated.

Faith's brother gave him a challenging look.

When in Rome…

Dale finally took the guy's work-roughened hand. He'd followed any number of odd customs in his travels not willing to offend a potential client or buyer. It didn't mean he'd have to like it, even if only a dinnertime prayer.

The mayor made a grand show of blessing the food. He had politician written all over him. Smooth and polished. Funny, no matter what size the pond, big fish were always going to act like big fish.

Dale's stomach rumbled. He hadn't eaten since lunch, a light meal served in the corporate limo on the way to the airport.

He felt a slight squeeze from Faith.

He glanced her way.

She looked as if she held back laughter. No doubt she'd heard his belly growl.

After the mayor's prayer, the noise level immediately escalated as lids came off serving platters and food was passed around.

"You're a hard man to get a hold of." Cord, the oldest brother, passed a bowl of steaming potatoes.

"Yes." No sense in denying it. Dale had ducked every call made from Jasper Gulch. But in the end, Julian had won. Dale was here, his father wasn't.

"Is your father planning to attend homecoming?" Cord asked.

"Not this time. He's traveling to Hong Kong." An excuse. His father never did what he didn't want to. Those responsibilities fell to Dale, and who was he to say no?

"Do you have any brothers or sisters who might come?" the younger sister asked. Julie was her name, and she resembled Faith. Both young women had slightly different shades of the rich auburn hair from their mother.

Dale passed the bowl to Faith. "Two half brothers, and no, they won't be joining me."

Faith's eyes went wide. "Would they come if they knew we've got a Massey-family float planned for the Thanksgiving Day parade?"

Julian hadn't said anything about Thanksgiving. Dale assumed it was only this weekend for their homecoming thing. "I won't be staying. I've got business in New York."

Faith shared a look with her sister. "But it's Thanksgiving. Don't you take vacation and spend time with your family?"

Dale gave her a grim smile. "Not if I can help it."

Her pretty mouth dropped open and she lowered the bowl of potatoes and whispered, "I'm sorry."

"For what?"

Faith shook her head. "I assumed you'd celebrate like a normal person, you know, with parents and turkey and all the trimmings. Only here, in Jasper Gulch."

He chuckled. *Normal.* What was that? "I enjoy the luxury of going where I please for holidays."

"All alone?" She bit her lip.

He leaned toward her and lowered his voice. "Not always."

Her eyes widened. He'd flustered her again.

Well, what did she expect?

He passed a bowl and glanced at her once more. Faith Shaw looked sorry for him. He had everything money could buy. Whatever he wanted was his for the asking. What did she think he needed that she'd look at him with such pity?

He glanced around the table. Did anyone notice his conversation with Miss Shaw? No. Faith's family was busy eating and talking.

"You might find our homecoming event interesting," Cord said to him.

Dale doubted that, but he didn't want to appear rude. "Yeah?"

"The founders of Jasper Gulch, your great-great-grandfather and mine, buried a time capsule a hundred years ago that will be on display. In it were blueprints of what is now city hall and pretty extensive city planning documents, among other period items and photos."

Dale nodded. Those plans might actually be worth a look. "Interesting."

"Someone else thought so, too, since the time capsule was stolen back in July. But it was finally found a couple of weeks ago. Cal Calloway said it had been abandoned by Beaver Creek Bridge," Faith's sister said. "Cal's our deputy sheriff."

"Is that so?" Dale's curiosity waned. He glanced down the table and spotted the mayor sharing a look with his wife.

The man caught his eye and coughed. "We're a safe community, Dale. Personally, I think the culprit who stole the time capsule has left town."

Faith's eyes widened. "You think maybe it was Pete Daniels?"

The mayor shrugged. "Stands to reason when the capsule pops up after he's gone. But I guess we'll never know for sure. The important thing is the capsule was found with all that history intact. Things have certainly quieted down, too. We can all be thankful for that."

Dale nearly laughed at the serious nods given around the Shaw table. Was the biggest crime in Jasper Gulch this stolen time capsule? Probably some kid's prank.

Faith leaned his way. "Pete Daniels is sort of our town's troublemaker."

Dale matched her serious tone. "I see."

Yeah. That cleared it up.

Dale sighed. It was only a few days. He'd leave in a few days and his world would return to normal. *His normal.* And it couldn't come soon enough.

The next morning, Faith poured orange juice into a glass and looked at her father. Jackson Shaw had been grumpy the last couple of months and it was no wonder. The pressure from a six-month-long centennial celebration would wear on anyone. Being mayor of a small town that needed big results crushed heavy.

Good thing her dad had broad shoulders. Cord said he'd finally agreed that Jasper Gulch needed to grow to not only survive but flourish.

She watched him rub his temples. "You okay, Dad? Didn't you sleep well?"

Her father sighed. "I slept just fine."

She didn't believe him. Dark smudges hung under his eyes and he hadn't even touched his favorite sweet roll.

"Good morning." Dale Massey entered the dining room dressed in a suit. A suit! Shirt, tie, jacket, all in shades of olive. What man wore a color like that unless his clothes were army fatigues?

Faith stared.

He gave her one of his slow smiles that felt like a caress. "Something wrong?"

A man shouldn't be allowed to smile like that!

"You're dressed awful..." Faith stammered, "...awfully fine this morning."

"I've got a meeting at Lone Peak ski resort." Dale poured himself a cup of coffee from the carafe on the buffet as if he owned the place.

Obviously Dale didn't know that people didn't dress like that around here. Maybe he was meeting with a fancy client on vacation. But then, they wouldn't dress up like that, either. Not while on vacation.

"It snowed there overnight." Her father steepled his fingers and stared her down.

Faith knew what he was getting at. Dale wouldn't make it through the mountains in that rental car. He might do fine on the interstate, but once he hit the back roads, he'd get stuck for sure. "Dale, you can take my car. It has all-wheel drive and chains in the back."

Dale looked confused about the chains. "Thank you. Unfortunately, you're not authorized to use the lemon."

"Oh, that's okay. I can use my mom's car if I need to go anywhere."

"Faith." Her father's eyes briefly closed. She'd seen that look a dozen times growing up. It was his you-should-know-better look. "Take him there. Dale's our guest."

Dale gave her a wary glance before zeroing back in on her father. "I'm sure I'll be fine—"

"These mountain passes can be tricky this time of year. Faith knows the way and a shortcut, to boot." Her father gave her a nod that said arguing would be fruitless. "Adam and Austin will see to your chores."

Faith held her breath before letting it back out. She could refuse, but that wouldn't go over well with her father. Not when she still lived under his roof. And she'd look foolish in front of Dale. She'd planned to practice her violin, but she could do that tonight, so that was not the best excuse for declining. Butterflies in her stomach were even worse. Besides, that reaction played right into her father's matchmaking hands.

She wasn't interested in a guy like Dale Massey. Attracted? Who wouldn't be? She'd seen his taut abs outlined by the skimpy undershirt he wore. She glanced at *their guest*. "I need to drop by the bank on our way. How much time do you have?"

"Plenty." Dale sipped his coffee.

In other words, that meeting waited for him. Nice. The world revolved around Dale Massey's schedule. "Then I can eat breakfast."

"Take your time." Another sip.

"Have a seat, Dale." Her father gestured toward the table. "Sandy made a frittata but if you'd like something else, say the word. The boys have already eaten, but there's plenty."

"Sandy's a friend and our housekeeper and also a knitter for Julie's business," Faith explained while she loaded her plate from the chafing dishes on the buffet.

He gave her a bored look. "Coffee's fine."

Faith went back to the business of filling her plate. Dale would wish he'd have eaten these fixings after they were in the car for an hour-plus drive to Lone Peak. She made a mental note to stuff a few granola bars in her purse before they left. Then she sat down across from Dale, ignored his surprise at the heaping portion on her plate and dug in.

Dale watched Faith kiss the mayor's forehead.

"Bye, Daddy. Not sure when we'll be back." She sounded genuinely considerate. Spoiled, maybe? No. He knew spoiled, and Faith Shaw wasn't that.

"Take your time. And fill up your gas tank before you leave Jasper Gulch."

"Will do." She waited for him by the doorway. "Ready?"

Dale gathered his thoughts. "Yes."

She gave him a once-over. "Don't you have a different coat? Or boots?"

"This coat is warm, and these are my boots." They were Gucci and comfortable.

Her eyes lowered in a knowing look. "You've never been to Lone Peak."

"No." Dale wasn't a ski nut like Eric, his half brother. He never had the time or the inclination. "How'd you guess?"

"You're a bit overdressed." By her tone, he knew she wasn't giving him a compliment. "I'll get some real boots for you."

"But we'll be in the car." Dale looked out the window as he followed her. The sun shone through puffy white clouds in a blue sky. Not a flake of snow at the Shaw spread.

"Out here, it's best to be prepared."

"For what?" Dale waited for her as she dived into a large walk-in closet.

She looked at him as if he lacked a brain. "We're driving through the mountains. We could go off the road, get stuck in snow. Any number of things. The ski resorts have snow. The peaks always have snow. Your feet will freeze if we have to walk anywhere."

"I see." Dale owed the mayor a debt of gratitude for making Faith drive. He'd never given a breakdown or accident a single thought. Probably not wise to drive around this desolate area alone. He'd already learned cell coverage was spotty at best.

"Try these." She tossed a pair of thick boots his way. They were huge lace-up things with felt liners.

Dale slipped off one sleek leather boot and stuck his foot inside. "Yeah, they fit."

She smiled. "I figured you were closer to Adam's size than Austin's. You've got big feet."

He chuckled as he slid his foot back into his own shoe-boot. "So, how'd you end up so small compared to the rest of your family? Did they find you under a fern somewhere?"

She grinned. "That would explain a few things."

"Like what?"

"Like why I never want to leave this land. Shaw land is part of me, like, in my blood. You know?"

He didn't, but he nodded anyway as he watched her shrug into her own coat and pull on felt-lined boots that hit her midcalf and had fake fur along the top. He followed her out and climbed into the passenger seat of her little SUV.

The Shaws lived quite a ways out of town. Their driveway alone seemed like miles long. Lush green grass surrounding the house gave way to straw-colored grass that grew tall and spindly against the wire fencing. An immaculate spread of red barns and outbuildings, the property had to be worth a small fortune. Horses sauntered in their pasture, some following after Faith's SUV within their confined space.

Dale stared out the window as if transfixed by the purple mountains behind rolling hills dotted with evergreens. The clear blue sky held puffy white clouds that looked so huge and close enough to touch.

"It is beautiful land," he finally said.

"I think so." Faith nodded. "Different than New York, I imagine."

He chuckled and focused on Faith's driving the road ahead. She had a lead foot. "Very different. Although, the city sprawls with the same vastness. New York is huge and it's a city that never sleeps."

Faith shook her head. "I wouldn't like that. I look forward to my eight hours."

Dale had certainly received his share of sleep overnight and then some. He'd slept hard with none of the trouble that came with travel and hotel rooms.

Finally, Faith pulled into the bank on the corner of Shaw Boulevard and Main. Dale made a call on his cell during the short drive into town. He'd gotten through to his office and left a message on his father's voice mail that he was headed for the ski resort meeting. He'd give him an update later.

Faith parked, got out and then peeked her head back inside. "Want to come in? There's a picture of your great-great-grandpa hanging on the wall in there."

Dale checked his phone. No new messages. "Silas?"

Faith nodded.

"Yes. I'd like to see that."

Despite the warm morning sunshine, there was a distinct chill in the air. He glanced at those awful boots tossed in the backseat. No way.

They walked toward the glass doors of a building that blended in with the rest. Same storefront look with a simple facade. It didn't look old. Not like the city hall building he'd seen when he first drove into town. In fact, that place looked more like a bank than this one.

"Hi, Faith." A man close to his own age and height opened the door for her as he exited the bank. His smile was warm and welcoming. The word *easygoing* came to mind.

"Pastor Ethan, good morning." She stopped short and Dale nearly ran into her. Again. "This is Dale Massey—he's come to represent one of the founding families for homecoming."

The guy extended his hand. "Nice to meet you."

Dale shook it. Pastor Ethan looked more like a well-groomed surfer than a minister. He had relaxed casual nailed. Faith could do worse. "Likewise."

"I'm showing him around," Faith said with a sheepish smile.

"Great. Yeah, well, have a nice day." The minister nodded and walked on. No jealousy there.

Dale followed Faith inside. "That's your boyfriend?"

Faith shook her head and laughed. "No."

"But your mom said—"

"Just talk. There's too much talk in this town, especially these days. All I did was bid on his picnic basket and next thing I know, folks were guessing the date."

"You did what?"

"Bid on his picnic basket, you know, at the fair."

He was lost.

Faith's eyes widened with pitiful mirth. "You've never been to a small-town fair."

"No." Why'd she make it sound as if he'd missed something important?

They walked inside and another man, short and stocky in a gray suit with a bad comb-over from premature hair loss, approached them. He, too, had a wide smile for his compact chaperone. And maybe a little more interest, too. "Morning, Faith."

Faith smiled in return. "Dale, this is Wilbur Thompson. He manages the bank. Mind if I show him the picture of Silas Massey in the safe-deposit-box room?"

"Certainly. Wait—are you Dale Massey? Of Massey International?" Wilbur turned to him with gleaming eyes.

Dale gave a quick nod. "I am."

"Nice article in *Fortune,* by the way. Mr. Massey, are you staying in town? If so, we'd be honored to set up a temporary account for you to use. It'll only take a few moments."

"I'm all set."

Wilbur gave him a shrewd look. "Well, here's my card if you change your mind."

"Thanks." Dale pocketed it. He wouldn't need it, wouldn't use it, either.

"That's my great-great-grandfather." Faith pointed to the portrait in the lobby. "Ezra Shaw."

He looked at the stocky man in the picture with a handlebar mustache.

Faith stood next to him. "My middle name is Elaine, after Ezra's wife."

Faith Elaine Shaw. He looked at her. She liked to chatter.

Her cheeks colored. "The safe-deposit-box room is this way."

He followed her across a hardwood floor that creaked. Every person, staff member and customer alike knew Faith and greeted her with warmth. They'd stop and chat, and Faith returned that same warmth with a grin or wave, or a quick caress to a chubby toddler's cheek. She was the mayor's daughter, after all, but she didn't seem a bit affected by that. These were natural actions.

Once they were in the safe-deposit room, Dale pointed out the obvious. "You talked to everyone in this place."

"Sorry. You said time wasn't an issue." She shrugged. "I grew up here. Went to school with these people, and babysat their kids when I was a teenager. Now, take a good look at that picture and tell me what you see."

Dale looked up at the canvas of a man who looked neither young nor old. His hair looked darker and longer and Silas wore a beard that covered half his face. "A creepy version of me or my father even. Didn't anyone use a razor back then?"

"He's not creepy," Faith defended, and then stared at the canvas with him. "I think he's kind of handsome."

Dale stared at her. "You're crazy."

She giggled. "Silas was a gold miner and a brave one, at that, so I've heard. He and my great-great-grandfather founded this town and opened this bank with their gold. Well, back then, the bank was what is now city hall." Dale stared at the portrait, only partially hearing what Faith said. This man was his relative. His history. Silas Massey had shrewd eyes that looked out from the canvas with intelligence. He was probably a good businessman. So, what made the guy head east if he had everything going for him right here?

"Why isn't his portrait out front in the lobby beside Ezra's?"

Faith shrugged. "I don't know. Silas has been in here ever since I can remember."

"Why'd he leave?"

"I don't know that, either. No one really does. Oh, there were rumors that the two fought over a claim. Who knows? It was a long time ago."

Dale glanced at the portrait of his great-great-grandfather again. An odd connection to the man resonated even though Dale knew very little about him. Silas might have been a wild gold miner, for all he knew, but he'd laid the groundwork for Massey International, a business Dale's grandfather started and Julian perfected.

Dale did his best to grow it, but on this trip, it was all about protecting it. Dale didn't stand for money pits. Purchasing an office space for his brother Eric might end up a giant sinkhole if the place was never used.

Chapter Three

Faith stood in line and tried not to overhear the conversation in front of her between the bank teller and Robin Frazier. Robin had moved to Jasper Gulch over the summer to work on some kind of genealogy project for her thesis.

Faith felt bad for the young woman who'd lost her ATM card in the bank's machine and faced the firing squad before getting it back.

"I need to reference your driver's license, Miss Frazier." The teller, one of Nadine Shaw's good friends, had a voice that carried. "Okay, now sign here please, exactly as on your card, Robin Elaine Frazier."

Faith's attention snagged on the middle name. Same as hers.

"I know it's you, hon, but I still have to jot down your ID number for documentation." The teller handed back Robin's ID and ATM card.

Finally finished, with plastic in hand, Robin turned, looking frazzled.

"Hi, Robin." Faith stepped forward and whispered, "I couldn't help but overhear. We've got the same name."

Robin blinked a couple of times and then rubbed the dark mole under her eyebrow. "Same name?"

Faith quickly explained, "My middle name is *Elaine,* same as yours. Mine comes from my great-great-grandmother." She pointed at Ezra's portrait. "His wife."

"Yes, that's right. Ezra married Elaine. Pretty common name, though." Robin still looked a little rattled.

And Faith had overstepped her bounds by admitting that she'd listened to the entire conversation. She didn't want Robin to think she was nosy and touched the woman's arm. "I'm sorry, I didn't mean to intrude."

"No worries." Robin smiled.

"Good."

"Faith Elaine, you stepping up here or what?" The teller used the same tone in her voice as Faith's mom when she was in trouble.

"Yes, ma'am." Faith gave Robin a mock look of fright. "My turn."

Robin laughed and waved goodbye.

Faith finished her business of a deposit of the last paycheck she'd receive for a while. As a violinist in

Bozeman, she wasn't needed until after Christmas when the regular concert series started up again. Only primary musicians who'd been around a lot longer than Faith played at the upcoming Christmastime ballet.

She glanced behind her. Wilbur bent Dale's ear and the real estate mogul looked bored to tears until a young blonde bombshell walked right up to both men and smiled.

Faith clenched her teeth. There was no denying the appreciation in Dale's eyes when he looked at the beautiful Lilibeth Shoemaker.

"Here you go, Faith. And watch out, Lilibeth is checking out your fella." The teller finished her deposit transaction with a smile.

"He's not mine, but thanks." Faith scanned the balance on her receipt and fought the urge to keep walking right out the door. That would be rude. And show her weakness.

She joined the cozy party of three.

Lilibeth gave her a sweet smile. "Why, Faith, I was just asking Mr. Thompson if he needed Christmas help this year and come to find out we have a real live Massey in our midst."

"Yeah, we do." Faith gripped her purse strap so tight her fingers curled into a fist around the leather.

Lilibeth placed her hand on Dale's arm and leaned toward him with a ridiculously brilliant smile. "Are there any more of you?"

"Not here." He looked amused.

Lilibeth made a pouty face. "Too bad."

Dale looked at Faith. "Ready?"

"Yep." She tamped down a heady feeling of triumph when she saw Lilibeth's mouth drop slightly open. "Bye, and thanks, Wilbur."

"Of course, of course." The manager fixed his attention back on the girl. "Now, Lilibeth, what hours can you work?"

As she left the bank with Dale, Faith let loose a soft laugh.

"What's so funny?" Dale opened the driver's-side door for her.

"Nothing." Faith shook her head. "It's nothing."

He climbed into the passenger seat. "Something to do with the prom queen in there?"

Not too many men gave Lilibeth the brush-off. Faith couldn't remember if Lilibeth had ever made it to prom queen, but the girl was furious when she didn't win the Miss Jasper Gulch beauty pageant. People wondered if she had been the one who stole the time capsule out of revenge. But over the past few months she seemed to have mellowed and had even helped out with the picnic basket auction. Most everyone now believed she was innocent.

Faith cocked her head. "She was trying to flirt with you and you shut her down."

"A lot of women flirt with me."

No doubt, but Faith still raised her eyebrows at such a conceited response. "And you don't flirt back?"

He gave her a silky smile that made her heart beat a notch faster. "Of course I do. But I have rules."

Faith let loose a snort of laughter. A flirt with a moral code. "What kind of rules could you possibly have?"

He looked genuinely offended. "First, they've got to be old enough to know better."

"Ah, well, that's sensible. Lilibeth's only nineteen." How could he tell? Faith couldn't believe they were having this conversation.

"And second." Dale's green eyes looked deadly serious. "They must be safe."

"Safe?" Faith scrunched up her face.

What on earth did he mean by that? What did he have to fear? Maybe Dale wasn't the heartbreaker type. He seemed too cold to get involved with a woman long enough for that. And too sophisticated, besides. She imagined that Dale Massey didn't like messy breakups. He struck her as something of a neat freak to boot. No doubt anything messy made him uncomfortable.

He nodded. "Safe."

"Huh." Faith started the car.

Did women throw themselves at him because of who he was as heir to the Massey empire? Probably. But he'd flirted with her. Did that mean she was safe? She swallowed hard on that disappointing thought.

No, wait. Safe was good. She should be happy with *safe*.

She glanced at his finely chiseled face. "Do you need anything before we leave town? More coffee, perhaps? There's a nice bakery across the street if you're hungry."

"No."

"I have granola bars in my purse. Let me know if you want one."

He gave her an amused look. "I'll keep that in mind."

What—too good for granola bars? Faith pulled out and hung a left onto River Road and then pulled into the corner gas station.

"Here—" Dale handed her his credit card "—have them fill it up. I got this." Then his phone vibrated and he answered it, already absorbed. "Dale Massey."

Faith took the card and flipped the inside lever to her gas cap and got out. This was his trip, after all; she'd gladly let him pay for her gas. She didn't know who he thought *they* were to pump it.

"Faith!"

She looked up as her friend since grade school, Marie Middleton, exited the minimart with a tall vanilla latte. Her favorite. "What's up?"

"Had to make a delivery of flowers."

"Really, who to?"

Marie gave her a look. "You know I can't tell you. Customer privacy policy."

"Awww, come on. Who are they from then? At least tell me that."

Marie looked around and then whispered, "Ellis Cooper."

Faith laughed.

The guy had run against her father in the last mayoral race. No doubt Ellis sent flowers to impress someone. With all the dignitaries in town for homecoming, the recipient could be anyone, really.

Ellis had championed the bridge fund to get votes, but Faith didn't buy his sincerity for the project. He'd be the kind of guy who'd want the bridge named after him once it opened. If he'd had the means to fund it, then take the name and the glory. But Cooper Bridge didn't have the same ring as good old Beaver Creek.

Marie squinted as she bent to look in Faith's car. "Who's the suit?"

Faith harnessed the gas nozzle back into the pump and waited for the receipt to print. "Dale Massey from New York."

"So, he finally showed, huh?"

"Yup." Faith ripped the paper.

"He's pretty hot." Marie grinned. "Where are you two going?"

"Lone Peak. Dad doesn't want him wandering

around the mountains by himself." Faith lowered her voice. "I mean, just look at him."

"Hmm. Not hard to do." Marie wiggled her fingers. "Have fun."

"Yeah, you, too."

Not what Faith had meant. Dale had pampered city boy written all over him. She climbed in behind the wheel and handed Dale his plastic along with the receipt.

He took it without looking at her or missing a beat of his phone conversation.

Faith pulled back onto Main Street and headed east out of town and toward the mountains while Dale talked on his phone about attorney fees.

After he'd ended his call, Dale stared out the window. Not exactly a talkative guy.

"Why not take that bridge? Seems like a more direct route."

Faith sighed. "The Beaver Creek Bridge has been out of commission forever."

"Why?"

Faith shrugged. "It's a sore spot with some people. My father included."

"What happened?"

"My great-aunt died when her car slid off the bridge into the rapids below. Her body was never found."

"That's the reason no one uses it?"

Faith gave another soft laugh. "It must sound silly

to a big-city guy like you, but Lucy Shaw's accident was substantial drama in little Jasper Gulch. Rumor had it she didn't want to marry the man her father had picked out, so maybe she drove off that bridge. Investigating the accident first closed it, but then folks didn't use it and the bridge fell into disrepair.

"We're trying to raise money, but haven't gotten close to what's needed for renovation. My brother Cord is on the town council and leading the charge. But, because my father would rather see it torn down, some folks side with him. Kinda funny that the time capsule was found near the bridge, considering the ruckus over it." She shrugged. "Jasper Gulch needs to grow regardless."

"Tax base drying up?"

Faith nodded. "Some businesses think they can't make it here with so few people. So, it's a vicious cycle. Kids leave for college or whatever and don't come back. That's why this centennial celebration is so important. It puts Jasper Gulch on the tourist map. Hopefully."

"With only one long way in and out, this town will get overlooked by tourists."

Again, Faith nodded. "One of the reasons for last month's Old-Tyme Wedding. Other than giving me a new brother-in-law and sister-in-law, the event gave folks a glimpse of what we have here. Hopefully more exposure to tourists than a website or looking at a map. The Bozeman TV spot got picked up nationally."

"I didn't see it."

Faith increased speed on the open stretch of road. "Fifty couples got married at once. Cord's got a copy of the ceremony. I can show you."

Dale's eyelids lowered with distaste. "That's okay."

Faith chewed her bottom lip. She must sound like a real bumpkin going on and on about her little town.

She glanced at Dale again.

He checked his phone, snorted and shoved it back in his pocket.

"No coverage out here. Probably none till we get to Lone Peak. I'm sure the resort has Wi-Fi." Why was he meeting someone way out here anyway?

Dale stared out the window. "This is desolate country."

Faith didn't think so. "I've always thought of it as vibrant and teeming with life."

"You want vibrant? Come to New York." Pride rang in his voice.

"No, thank you." Faith shook her head. "I tried city life once. It wasn't for me."

"Where?" His voice challenged.

"Seattle."

"Hmm. Cool city. Artsy."

She'd managed to impress him. A little.

Faith had discovered the ugly side of the arts and men who took advantage. Not willing to sell her soul, she packed up and came home. She'd never felt more like a naive country bumpkin than when she fell for her mentor in Seattle while trying to make something of her music. "Parts of it."

"What lured you there?" He gave her a slanted smile. "A man?"

"No." Faith laughed. "A job, but it didn't work out."

Dale gave her a long look but didn't dig. "For a girl who doesn't drink coffee, Seattle must have been a scary place."

"What makes you think I don't drink coffee?" They were in the mountains now, and Faith concentrated on the winding road.

"You only drank orange juice this morning."

"A small thing to notice." Faith shrugged.

"I'm in the business of noticing small things."

Faith's heartbeat picked up speed. So, the guy paid attention to details. But something about the silky softness of his voice made her wonder if she was the *small thing* he noticed.

Part of her hoped so.

And part of her didn't.

"Well, I drink coffee, but I'd had my fill before breakfast." She had to remember that she was *safe*.

It dawned on her that safe meant no threat of serious entanglement. She wasn't worth pursuit of anything more than flirtation. Not in the life of Dale Massey.

She shouldn't be surprised. She'd summed him up pretty good yesterday. And really, she wanted no part of a guy like him. The world was littered with them. So, why the nugget of hurt lodged in her heart?

Dale stared at the snow-covered mountains filled with people skiing, getting an early jump on the holiday. One of several resorts in the Big Sky area, this place shone like a gem in the warm Montana sunshine. This was the kind of place he was used to, and no doubt perfect for Eric to set up shop. Maybe then the kid would finally ease his way into the Massey real estate business. But Dale had his doubts.

He got out of the car and stretched his legs. The mayor had been right. His rental never would have made the drive here, not the way Faith had taken them, plus she'd shaved a good half hour in drive time going through the mountains instead of around them on the interstates.

He poked his head back into the interior. "I'm not sure how long I'll be, where do you want to meet?"

Faith shrugged. "Right here is fine."

"You're not going to stay in your car."

"I've got a good book, and the sun's shining. I'll be fine."

Dale shook his head and pulled out his wallet. "Take my credit card and buy whatever you want."

Her expressive eyes widened and she held up her hand. "Put that away. I am not using your card."

He'd offended her. "You let me buy the gas."

"That was different."

He tipped his head. What did she think he offered? "You should be compensated for your time. I'm taking up a good chunk of your day."

Faith shook her head and pulled out her book. "Forget it."

Letting the argument slide, he handed her his business card. "Here's my cell if you need to get a hold of me."

"I won't." She took the business card though, and then buried her nose in the pages of a paperback.

Dale chuckled as he walked away. He'd managed to ruffle Miss Shaw's pretty feathers. Women were fickle that way. Finding insult when he merely wanted to repay her for her time. If he'd wanted a more interesting transaction between them, he would have been candid. Dale didn't play games. Faith Shaw struck him as honest, too, but in a pure and simple sort of way. She wasn't the kind of girl for anything more than a pleasant flirtation.

By the time Dale finished touring the office space for sale, he knew it was technically perfect for their needs and exactly what his father had wanted. But Dale didn't jump on the offer. A gut feeling prevented him from purchasing the property—something he didn't know what to name other than a profound sense of dissatisfaction with the whole deal.

Instincts were a big part of what he did, so he knew when to listen. Today, he'd stand down and wait. He shook the guy's hand, promised to get back to him and walked away.

And then he called the office. "Jeannie, where are we with those closings scheduled for next week? On task? Good, put me through to my father's voice mail." Dale waited for the connection. Julian was on his way halfway across the world, but he'd still want an update. "Not confident on this property. I think we can do better."

Dale scanned the surrounding high-end shops. Faith had been correct in her assessment that he'd overdressed. There was money here, big money, but the atmosphere remained casual. Relaxed. Typical of a vacation resort.

Maybe she'd help him pick up a few things while they were here. Some jeans. He'd talk her into something for herself, too. He wouldn't mind seeing her dressed for an evening out. His stomach growled.

Lunch first, then shopping.

As he approached Faith's SUV, he found himself smiling. The driver's seat reclined and the window was open a crack for air, and Faith slept in the surprisingly warm sunshine. The paperback novel—a romance, he realized—lay open on her midsection.

Her long auburn hair draped the headrest, exposing a pretty expanse of white neck. He thought about kissing that skin. How could he not?

He nearly laughed when he thought of her indignant reaction when he'd offered her his credit card. What would she do if he kissed her? It might be worth it to find out.

With a soft creak of metal, he slowly opened her door, shaking his head that she'd left it unlocked. But his amusing idea died the moment he really looked at her. She was beautiful in a natural way, like raw sugar. Unrefined and sweet. Vulnerable. She was the mayor's daughter. His host. Making her pretty much off limits.

She sighed and shifted. Her lips were certainly tempting. Maybe too tempting.

Dale shook her shoulder instead. "Wake up, Sleeping Beauty."

Her eyes opened and Faith looked dreamy and soft. The corners of her wide mouth curled into a sleepy smile. "What time is it?"

"Time for lunch." His voice sounded oddly tender to his ears. He wanted to push back her hair but rested his hand on the car's roof. "Did I interrupt a good dream?"

Her blue eyes focused and she sat up with a start. Her book fell to ground.

Dale picked it up and handed it back to her.

Faith tossed the book in the backseat. "Sorry. The sun was so warm, I fell asleep."

He chuckled. "I noticed."

She blushed.

He held the door for her, liking this girl. Sure, she'd talked his ear off, but there was something open about her. Nothing disguised or put on. "Come on. The least I can do is buy you lunch."

Looking deliciously tousled, Faith slid out of the car and finger combed her hair. "Lunch, yeah. I could eat."

Dale couldn't ignore the avalanche of awareness coursing through him, making him light-headed. Hunger did that to a person. Despite not being a big morning eater, he shouldn't have skipped breakfast. These unsettling feelings were nothing more than hunger. Plain and simple.

Faith stifled a yawn as she slipped into the chair held out for her by the restaurant host. "Thank you."

The host nodded but didn't look impressed, with a pinched nose and thin smile.

Faith looked around. A casual place when it came to customer dress, but everything about it screamed expensive. A fancy wine collection covered one of the brick walls. White linen tablecloths complete with fresh flowers graced the tables. Yup, expensive.

Dale checked his phone and texted, oblivious to the disdainful looks he received from the maître d'.

Dale accepted the menu without a word. He was used to being waited on, probably in places even nicer than this.

"How'd your meeting go?" Faith couldn't take the silence, or the uncomfortable feeling that she'd crashed someone else's party.

He pocketed his phone. "Went well."

By the tight look on his face, she'd guess it didn't. "You don't look happy."

He flashed a smile, signaling a change of subject. "What do you say we do some shopping after we eat? You were right, I need casual clothes."

She frowned. He didn't want to talk business, and that was okay by her as long as they talked about something. Anything to keep her mind off the dream she'd had of him while sleeping in the car. "What are you looking to buy?"

"Jeans. Maybe some boots, so I don't have to use your brother's. There are quite a few shops here."

Faith snorted. "You'll pay through the nose."

He cocked an arrogant eyebrow. Money wasn't an issue.

Faith gulped her water. Then she looked him straight in his handsome face. "Can I ask a favor?"

"Name it."

She took a deep breath. "Would you shop in Jasper Gulch instead?"

"I didn't see a clothing store."

Faith grinned. "Our hardware store has a clothing

section. Boots, jeans, socks, shirts. Anything you might need for the outdoors or casual rugged living." She quoted their advertisement and then added. "The Walkers could really use the patronage."

Faith knew they'd increased their inventory because of the centennial celebrations, hoping to appeal to shoppers and increase business.

He narrowed his gaze, zeroing in on her again. "Sure. On our way back."

She twisted her napkin in her lap. "Great, thanks."

His green eyes softened. "You're welcome."

Faith shifted her attention to the menu, but the words blurred out of focus. She felt his gaze still on her. "What?"

"You really care about your town, don't you?"

Silly question. "Of course, why wouldn't I?"

"But you genuinely *care*. It's your nature, isn't it? Caring."

What was he getting at? And why did he look at her as if she was an interesting new toy? A plaything. Dale Massey probably discarded new toys as a kid once the novelty wore off and his interest waned. She wouldn't be surprised if he did the same thing as an adult.

Faith pulled out the big guns with ammo she knew from experience had the power to dampen a man's ardor in a hurry. "The Bible says love thy neighbor as thyself. In Jasper Gulch, that isn't too hard to do. Most of the time."

Dale's brow furrowed and then he laughed. It

was a deep, belly-rolling sound she'd never have expected to come out of a New York prince. "Nice move, Faith."

She stared at him.

"I'm trying to figure you out and you quote scripture. Good blocking maneuver."

No sense denying it. "Well, quit trying to figure me out."

"Why?"

Because you make me uncomfortable and my heart races when you smile. Because I dreamed of kissing you.

Faith didn't voice her thoughts. She didn't have to because the waiter dressed in a crisp white shirt and black pants chose that moment to arrive and take their orders.

Without hesitation, she asked for a well-done cheeseburger, fries and a pop. Dale did the same. Smiling at her with that secret-sharing smile all because they'd ordered the same thing. It made her stomach flutter. Ridiculous man! He poured on the charm a little too thick.

After the waiter left and returned with their soft drinks, Dale leaned forward. "Why don't you date your young minister? He seems like a nice guy."

"He is." Faith sipped her pop. "But he's not my type."

"What's your type?" The flirtatious glint was back in his eyes.

And that was a good thing. It meant she was safe.

Scripture always came to the rescue when needed. Faith tipped her head and raised her glass. "I'll let you know when I meet him."

Dale's smile grew wider.

And Faith's stomach dropped. She had a bad feeling she may have misspoken, because Dale Massey was exactly her type.

Chapter Four

Dale couldn't remember a time when he'd enjoyed a meal with a woman more. For one thing, Faith ate her food instead of picking at it. He didn't know where she put it all, but the girl could eat. If he had a dollar for every woman he'd been out with who ordered salad and then left it unfinished, he'd be an even richer man.

Faith was real. And rather charming, too, in an honest, chatterbox sort of way. A bright spot in an otherwise inconvenient errand.

"You sure you don't want to have a look around the stores while we're here?" Women loved to shop, right?

Faith shook her head. "No, no. I'm fine."

He glanced at her. She'd slipped out of her puffy jacket. She wore jeans and a sweater. A band of silver wrapped around her index finger and a watch encircled her wrist. "You're not much into frills, are you?"

Faith shrugged. "I like a nice dress now and then."

She wasn't giving anything away, but Faith Shaw was not playing hard to get. He'd seen that role before and this wasn't it. Dale knew he impressed most people, women in particular. So why was *this* woman indifferent to who he was but not what he was? He could tell she found him attractive. No surprise there. He found her attractive, too.

After the check had been paid and they walked side by side to the parking lot, Dale held out his hand. "Would you like me to drive?"

"Sure." Faith hesitated only a moment before handing over her keys.

"To the Jasper Gulch hardware store." He held the passenger-side door open for her.

She slipped in and buckled up. "Thanks."

He leaned toward her. "My pleasure."

She shook her head and laughed, making him want to try harder. Faith Shaw had poise, and a guard higher than most. Well, he was pretty good at scaling walls.

With one last glimpse of the mountains surrounding them, Dale tossed his cashmere coat over the backseat and then slid into the driver's side, adjusting the seat to accommodate the length of his legs. "Do you ever ski here?"

"I'm not much of a downhill skier, but I like cross-country and snowshoeing. I paddle my way around the ranch when we get a good snow, but I've been to Lone Peak before. There are beautiful trails here."

Dale imagined that was true. Although desolate, the scenery was postcard pretty. He pulled out onto the road mulling over what Faith had told him. Cross-country and snowshoes made sense. Faith Shaw kept her feet firmly planted on the ground.

Halfway to Jasper Gulch on the back road Faith had taken, Dale noticed an odd vibration in the steering wheel, followed by a consistent thump that grew louder. "Hear that?"

Faith's eyes widened. "You should pull over."

He did so, on a level stretch of road—if it could be called that. The entire pathway was white with packed snow. Evergreen trees lined the sides and they were dusted with the same. Clouds had crowded out the sun, making it feel much colder than before. And they hadn't seen another vehicle since leaving the resort. There was no one in sight.

Dale got out and looked at the car, recognizing the problem right away. "Flat tire."

Faith came around the front of the SUV to stand next to him. "Wonder why."

"Does it matter?" Dale pulled his phone out of his suit-coat pocket and tried looking up the nearest tow truck. His internet connection churned sluggishly.

"You won't get coverage here." Faith headed for the back of the vehicle. She opened the hatch and reached in, pulling out the spare tire and then the jack.

Dale watched her, phone in hand. "What are you doing?

"I'm going to change the tire."

"What about a tow truck?" He looked around the road. "Aren't there any emergency phones out here?"

Faith laughed. "No. Who are you going to call, anyway?"

Dale glanced at his phone. The circle timer still swirled. "Have you ever changed a tire before?"

"Yes. My father made sure I knew how before I left for college. I can do it."

Dale headed for the back of the truck, slipping as he went. His Gucci boots didn't have much traction. Fumbling in a duffel bag labeled Safety Kit, he found neon orange triangles and a couple of fat candles. He placed the triangles along the side of the road behind them and then carefully padded his way to the front of the car. He should put on his long wool coat, but it'd only get in the way and restrain his movement.

He reached inside to click on the hazard lights. "What are those candles for?"

"A heat source in case I go off the road. Never leave a car idling if you're stuck in a snowbank." Faith knelt on the snow-packed road and loosened the lug nuts of the driver's-side front tire with the crowbar that came with the jack. She looked as if she knew what she was doing.

"Here, let me help."

Faith glanced up at him. "You ever do this?"

"No." What kind of man was he that he couldn't change a tire? "But I can figure it out."

"You'll ruin your suit."

"I'll buy a new one."

Faith raised her eyebrows. "What about those shoes? They're showing water stains. Why don't you put on Adam's boots?"

He hated feeling useless, and she was right about his kid-leather boots. He'd ruin them, plus they were slippery on the surface of the road. "They're fine. Give me that jack."

She handed it over.

He looked at the tiny metal thing. "This is going to support the car?"

"It had better, considering it was made for it. Place the jack a little ways behind the tire, and then crank it up enough for me to wiggle off the wheel."

Carefully, he positioned the jack under the Honda. Using the lever and the crowbar, Dale got enough height for Faith to finish screwing off the lug nuts by hand. Then she tried to shimmy the wheel. It wouldn't budge.

"Don't reach underneath anything." Dale didn't trust that jack. "Here, let me do it."

She stepped aside. "Fine."

"There's the culprit. We ran over a nail." He wiggled the wheel and then pulled. It slipped off easier than expected and he backed up quickly, but his boots failed. Both feet came out from under him and he landed hard with the tire on top of his chest.

"Are you okay?" Faith stood looking down at him.

"Ah, yeah, fine." He groaned. The cold-packed snow melted, seeping into the seat of his trousers.

Faith giggled as she knelt down to pull the tire off him. Then she gasped. "Oh, no..."

He sat up and looked at the front of his suit. The tire had left a streak of grime from shoulder to hip. Ruined. He glanced at Faith.

Her blue eyes shone with unabashed amusement.

"It's not funny." But it was.

She burst into laughter.

He spread his arms wide. "This is one of my favorite suits."

And that made her laugh even harder. "It's downright ugly, if you ask me."

He grinned. "I'll have you know that I dated a cousin to the royal family in this suit."

"Really?" Faith wrinkled her nose. "Was it serious?"

He laughed at her wide-eyed innocence. "I don't do serious."

"Oh."

He tried to stand.

"Here." She reached out her hand.

He looked at it and then at her. Petite came to mind. Then crazy. "Yeah, like you're going to leverage me into standing."

"I'm no weakling."

"Neither am I." The last thing he needed was to pull her down with him if he slipped again.

He made an awkward show of getting up off the cold ground. She stifled a giggle with the palm of her hand.

Nice.

He managed to remain upright while he hauled the flat tire into the back of Faith's SUV. No need to worry about more dirt. His suit was toast. The temporary replacement tire lay on the ground waiting to be popped on and tightened. He managed to complete that task, too, without losing his balance.

"Step back," he ordered as he lowered the jack.

Faith folded her arms and waited, watching him silently.

He stood, whipped off his suit jacket and wiped his hands with it. Then he balled up the garment and looked around.

"Don't even think about leaving that behind."

"It's made of natural fibers, it'll break down." Did she think he'd really litter real garbage?

She snorted contempt. "Give it here and I'll throw it in the back. You still want to drive?"

"Yes." He tossed her the jacket and slipped into the driver's seat and started the engine. He needed to feel in control of something.

Flicking the switch for heated seats, he hoped his

backside would dry. And thaw. Man, he was cold. He cranked the heat.

Faith climbed in.

"Ready?" he asked.

She leaned toward him, inspecting his face.

"What?"

"You've got grease under your chin." She reached into the glove compartment and pulled out a wad of napkins. "Hold still."

He jerked his head out of reach and glanced in the rearview mirror. "Where?"

She grabbed his chin and pulled his face toward her. "Quit or you'll get the collar of your shirt messed up."

"I don't care about my shirt." He didn't fight her, though. The grip she had on his chin was strong.

She concentrated on wiping under his chin.

He watched her. Her eyelashes were ridiculously long.

"You've got a glob of grease right here." Leaning over the console that separated their seats, Faith rubbed the skin below his ear with a rough napkin.

"Are you done?" He tipped his head down and breathed in the soft scent of her wrist.

She looked up at him and her big blue eyes widened. Innocence. Maybe that's what drew him to her. All the more reason to stay away. She looked too innocent to go there. But they were so close. And some habits were hard to ignore.

Dale's instincts kicked in. He lowered his head and brushed his lips against hers. Nothing more than a brief taste. That's all he was after. That's all he could possibly go after.

But then Faith's response surprised him and before Dale knew what he was doing, he'd wrapped his arms around her. Too late, he realized there was nothing safe about this woman. On a lonely stretch of narrow road in the middle of the mountains, they were in her car alone. Dale shivered. No, it was more like a shudder from the inside out. Had to be the cold, not the woman. He quaked right down to the soles of his useless boots and pulled away.

Faith blinked at him like a deer caught in headlights. Stunned. Then she smiled. "Wow. You're really good at that."

"I'm good at a lot of things." He stared at her.

She blushed, making the scatter of freckles across her nose and cheeks stand out even more.

Was *she* toying with him? He didn't think so. She'd kissed him as if he meant something to her. Like she cared. And that was a dangerous place to be. He ran his hand through his hair and tried to get his bearings. "Look, Faith, uh, I'm sorry about that."

"Now you've got a smear of dirt on your forehead." She reached up, napkin in hand, completely ignoring him. Ignoring what had happened between them.

What had happened? He wasn't quite sure.

Dale took it from her, looked in the mirror and scrubbed.

"Thank you for changing the tire, by the way."

"You're welcome." He crumpled up the napkin and tossed it at her feet where the others had been thrown.

He looked at her.

She gave him another smile.

The woman could really smile. It lit up her whole face and did something to him. Dale might as well have slipped and fallen again. That same unbalanced feeling had him gripping the steering wheel.

"If we go now, we can make it to the hardware store before they close."

"Yeah." He checked his mirrors. No one. For miles. He was all alone with a girl who'd thrown him for a loop.

He pulled away from the side of the road with less speed than a grandmother. He couldn't get his bearings. A trip to Bozeman's airport made a lot more sense than traveling to the Jasper Gulch hardware store. But he was here for a reason, and there was no use backing out now.

He sighed.

"You okay?" Faith's voice was soft and quiet.

Finally, she'd acknowledged that something might be wrong. All wrong. And why was she so calm?

He cleared his throat. "Fine. Maybe a little worried about what kind of jeans your hardware store carries."

"Good ones, Dale. Jasper Gulch only carries the good ones made to last."

"Let's go, then." Dale pressed the gas a little harder.

Nothing lasted. Not jeans, and especially not relationships. His father had proved that with three sons from three different ex-wives. He glanced at Faith Shaw, who might be one of Jasper Gulch's good women. She deserved a man who'd last for the long haul.

That wasn't him.

Good thing he wasn't staying long. The sooner he got out of Jasper Gulch, the better. He'd do his Massey duty at the homecoming and then split. Until then, he'd keep his hands and lips far away from Miss Faith Elaine Shaw.

"Try these. Every cowboy I know wears them." Faith handed Dale a couple of pairs of jeans to try on.

"Thanks." He disappeared into the fitting room.

Faith leaned against the wall and nearly sank to the floor. What had she been thinking, kissing Dale like that? She couldn't stop reliving it, remembering the feel of it, the taste. Was it possible to fall in love at first kiss?

Dale had apologized.

She had to own that that had surprised her. After she'd kissed him back, Faith had scriptures lined up like buckets of cold water just in case. But she hadn't needed them. Dale had backed away quicker than a colt feeling his first saddle.

Why?

Faith closed her eyes. She shouldn't care about the answer. They were worlds apart. He'd never stay in Jasper Gulch and she'd never leave. Not that he'd offer. Men like him didn't offer anything proper. He'd said so himself that he didn't do serious relationships.

Knowing that, why in the world had she kissed him? Hadn't she learned her lesson in Seattle? And why had he apologized for kissing her?

Why?

"I don't know." Dale exited the dressing room with a pair of prewashed jeans that fit him just right. He turned a couple of times, looking in the mirror.

"I do. Buy them."

He gave her a quick look.

"Now all we have to do is find you a couple of decent shirts." She wandered away to rifle through the sweatshirts and thermals hanging on a circle rack.

"I have plenty of shirts." He stood behind her.

"Patronage, remember?" Faith whispered, trying to calm her jitters. Did he have to stand so close?

"Are you folks finding what you're looking for? Oh, Faith, I didn't see you."

Of course not. Dale practically hovered over her. She replaced a red thermal shirt and smiled. "Hi, Mike. This is Dale Massey, in need of clothes."

Dale extended his hand. "I ruined mine today."

Mike laughed at the stained olive button-down. "So I see. My wife can help with flannels. We got some new ones in today."

"Let me at 'em." Faith bustled toward his wife, Gale-Ann, hanging up plaids and checks on another rack.

Dale could afford to drop a few bucks and she'd saved him a fortune by diverting his shopping spree here. Not that he cared. Did he care, *really* care, about anything?

"Handsome fella you've got there, Faith," Gale-Ann whispered.

"He's not mine," she whispered back.

Dale sure had felt like hers when he'd kissed her, though. She wouldn't mind seeing Dale Massey dressed like one of them. In her dream this afternoon, he'd been one of them. And he *had* been hers.

"Hello there, Miss Faith."

She turned at the well-known sound of that craggy voice.

Ninety-six-year-old Rusty Zidek sauntered toward them, his worn cowboy boots shuffling against the wide-plank floors of the shop. He tipped his soft brown cowboy hat toward Dale. "Howdy, wrangler."

"Rusty, this is Dale Massey. Here for homecoming."

The old man whistled and then slapped his hat against his thigh. "Well, I'll be! A real live Massey. Staying at Shaw Ranch, I presume?"

"I am."

"Good hospitality there." Rusty gave her a nod. "I was too little to know your great-great-grandpa before he up and left, but I could tell you stories about him that'd turn you sideways."

Dale glanced at her before extending his hand. "Nice to meet you, Rusty."

Rusty took it and pumped hard. His easy smile crinkled his leathery skin and made the tips of his long gray mustache bounce. "You talk like a regular eastern greenhorn!"

Again, Dale looked at her for direction. Or maybe it was translation. Rusty wasn't talking Greek!

"He's from New York," Faith explained.

"Don't I know it. Silas struck out for there a long time ago. Must suit you, son. You look like you could wrangle a bull in no time."

"The only bull Mr. Massey has probably been close to is that bronze statue guarding Wall Street." Faith imagined he could *wrangle* stocks pretty well.

"She's right. No bulls." Dale nodded.

Rusty laughed and slapped the back of Dale's shoulder covered in the ugly olive-green-colored shirt. "You lift weights?"

Faith rolled her eyes.

"Tennis," Dale said. "And some racquetball."

Rusty choked on his chew. "Tennis? That's a girl's game."

"Not the way I play."

Faith glanced at Dale. Tennis had always seemed like a gentleman's sport, but the tone of Dale's voice was downright sinister. "Remind me never to play you in tennis."

"I'd go easy on you." He gave her that silky smile that drizzled over her like melted chocolate, rich and sweet but bad.

Rusty looked at them both and grinned, revealing his gold tooth. "Well, I'll let you two young'uns get back to yer shopping. Funny sort of date, if you ask me. See you at the homecoming."

"Bye, Rusty." Faith waved, not bothering to correct him. This was no date.

"Wow." Dale watched Rusty head into the tool section.

"What?"

"Is he for real?"

"As real as they get. Rusty Zidek is sort of a living monument here in Jasper Gulch. He was born here shortly after the town's founding and never really left except to play baseball." She pulled out a forest-green flannel for Dale to try on. "How about this one?"

He checked his watch. "Pick a couple and let's go. I've got work to do yet."

"What's your size?"

"Check." He stripped off that ugly green shirt of his and handed it over.

"Oh. Okay." She tried not to stare.

Dale wore another one of those skintight, silky looking undershirts that strained against his arms and shoulders. The guy had some guns. All that from tennis? Rusty was right. Dale looked as if he could wrangle a bull in no time.

"We good?" He snapped his fingers.

Faith jerked back to reality with a flood of heat to her cheeks. She knew when a man was done shopping. She had brothers whose patience suddenly snapped, too. Maybe Dale didn't do his own shopping.

So then, who did? Boy, she sure didn't like the green-eyed-monster feelings brought on by thoughts of another woman doing Dale's shopping. Really, what had gotten into her?

"Ah, yeah. Boots. They're over there if you want to try on a pair. I'll gather the shirts and meet you at the register."

He put his hands up in surrender. "I'm done. You can pick them out."

She watched him hightail it into the dressing room. He came back out wearing those awful trousers and his tan coat over his undershirt and he had his cell phone plastered against his ear. Did he never give that thing a rest?

She tromped into the stall he'd exited and gathered up the jeans he'd strewn all over. Okay, Dale Massey wasn't that much of a neat freak. Fine, she'd get the boots, since evidently it was up to her to pick out what he'd buy.

Since when had she become his assistant? If that's what rich men's assistants did—clean up messes left behind by their lofty bosses.

Faith tamped down her irritation. At least he was buying clothes here at her request. He'd come here for her. And maybe once Dale got out of those stuffy suits, he'd relax a little. But a relaxed Dale was bound to be even more attractive. And dangerous.

She got the feeling that he needed to relax. Something about the iron control of his expressions, the way he held himself firmly in check, made her wonder if he wasn't always on guard. That guard had slipped when he'd kissed her, though. He'd been affected by their embrace.

Faith grabbed a pair of boots and headed for the register. There was more than mere attraction bubbling between them. Was Dale Massey worth her digging deeper to see if there might be something real and maybe even lasting there? She aimed to find out.

Chapter Five

Leaving the hardware store, Dale was carrying several bags toward Faith's car when his phone buzzed. Shifting bags, he picked up. "Dale Massey."

"Dale? Where are you? I called your office, and Jeannie said you were in Montana."

"Yes, Mom, I'm in Montana." He looked at Faith and handed her a couple of bags to load into the back. "I'll be here for a couple of days."

"Where's your father?"

"Hong Kong."

"I didn't get my alimony check."

Dale clenched his jaw tight. Why did he have to hear about it? Julian had his own assistant, his own lawyer, too, but every month his mother pulled him into the middle, rattling on about his father's tardiness in payment. His father always paid late. It was Julian's way of demonstrating who had the control. His mother knew that.

"I'm sure it's on its way soon." Why couldn't she leave him out of it?

"It better be in my account before I leave."

Dale knew this game and didn't feel like playing. Ronna, his mother, wanted him to ask where she was going. "I'm sure you'll get it soon."

"I won't be home all next week." Her voice lilted, begging him to inquire.

He glanced at Faith, who'd slipped into the driver's seat of her car and started the engine. She'd parked close to the storefront in one of the diagonal spaces that bordered Main Street. A couple of women on horseback tethered their animals to a railing in front of a diner and then went inside. Now, *that* wasn't a sight he was used to seeing.

"Okay, Mom. I've got to go." He pulled the collar of his coat closer to ward off the chilly late-afternoon air.

"Don't you want to know where I'm going?" Ronna asked.

Dale shook his head. He never won with her. "Sure. Where are you going?"

"With friends to New Hampshire to ski."

"Great. Have fun."

"When you get back to the office, check on that deposit, would you?"

"Sure." He sighed. Ronna would never call, herself, hating to appear in need of the money.

"Dale?"

"Yes."

"Be careful out there." A hint of real concern swirled in her voice.

"Thanks, Mom. You, too." He slipped the phone back into his pocket and climbed into the passenger seat. "Sorry about that."

Faith waved his apology aside. "No problem. Everything okay with your mom?"

"Same as ever." He had run interference for his parents for as long as he could remember. The middleman between their lives and payments. "She called to let me know she'd be skiing with friends in New Hampshire next week."

Faith smiled, but a frown furrowed her brow. "She called you all the way from Hong Kong to tell you that?"

"My mother's not in Hong Kong."

"She didn't go with your father?" Faith obviously thought all marriages stayed together or she wouldn't have asked such a ridiculous question.

"My parents are divorced, so no."

"Oh. That's too bad."

"I suppose."

As Faith backed up, Dale looked down the street. Both ends of town had spectacular views of the distant mountain ranges that surrounded this big valley. Beyond the small used-car lot, he spotted a for-sale sign in front of a commercial property.

"What is that building beyond the car-sales place?"

"That's the Jenkins building. Used to be the newspaper office, but that moved into a smaller storefront. Businesses have been in and out of there ever since."

"Impressive views."

Faith nodded. "Yeah, we're pretty much surrounded by mountain ranges. Tobacco Root is toward the northwest, the Madison Range is east and we drove through them on our way to the ski resort. Then Snowcrest and Gravelly ranges are south of here."

"Pretty isolated though."

Faith shrugged. "I'm used to it."

Dale understood his father's choice to set up shop for Eric, but Jasper Gulch had amazing views that didn't quit. A far different atmosphere from Lone Peak. Jasper Gulch was not high end, but quaint. The difference between real life and the escapism of resort living.

Of course, that could all change if tourists descended on this little town as Faith said they aimed for. Curious, but he hoped they didn't lose sight of what they had here.

Jasper Gulch was a diamond in the rough.

Much like the woman next to him.

His phone buzzed again with a text message. He pulled it out and texted back.

"You're never far from that phone, are you?" Faith asked.

"Not if I can help it."

She made a face. "Not me. I carry one for emergencies, but that's pretty much it. But then, I don't have a business to run."

It dawned on him that not once had he seen her with a phone. "It's something I rely on and it's an efficient use of my time."

She shrugged. "What about downtime? You know, like vacations and stuff."

He gave her a crooked grin. "Vacations might be out of the office, but the phone goes with me. I have to be connected. Time is money."

Faith laughed then. "And money can be a waste of time."

Dale opened his mouth to ask what she meant by that, but his phone buzzed again.

Dale glanced out of the guest-bedroom window. Clouds had covered the moon and stars. It was dark outside. Darkness like he'd never seen before. Pitch-black. Sure, a distant light shone from the barn, and a small cottage lit from within sat on the hillside, but darkness blanketed everywhere else.

He rubbed his forehead and retreated to the desk where his laptop lay poised and his phone charged. He had work to do. Work he couldn't concentrate on. He'd excused himself after dinner from the masses of Shaws with paperwork as his excuse. That, and he couldn't keep his gaze from straying toward Faith all evening.

Fresh as a mountain stream, she'd bubbled through dinner about their adventure with the flat tire and shopping at the hardware store. He'd caught a couple of hopeful glances exchanged between the mayor and Nadine. And a hard look from Faith's brother Cord. Good thing Faith had left out the most disturbing part of their day or Dale might be facing a shotgun.

He never should have kissed her. Amazing as it had been, Dale wasn't about to play fast and loose with Faith Shaw. He had a hunch that keeping it casual might be tough. She had a sweetness he didn't want to sour when it came time to part ways. And that time always came.

Faith didn't seem too affected by their kiss, as if what happened hadn't mattered. But it mattered to him and that troubled him even more.

He glanced at the clothes Faith had picked out for him from the hardware store that now lay scattered on the bed. He hadn't bothered to put them away. Not much of a jeans guy, he had to admit the brand she'd recommended was comfortable, if a little looser in the seat than what he was used to. He looked down at those jeans he wore with a sweater and checked his watch.

Maybe a walk outside would clear his restless mind.

He grabbed his phone then slipped into the lace-up boots and the rugged barn coat Faith insisted he had to have. If nothing else, she'd said he would need a reminder of his heritage in Montana when he returned to New York.

He'd never thought much about his family's history until now. He'd always looked toward the future. He wanted to make the Massey empire a grand legacy he could leave to his half brothers to carry on. He'd never have kids of his own. He'd no desire to marry only to end up divorced over and over like his father. His mother had reminded him often enough how much like Julian he was, and Ronna's words had rooted deep. What his mother didn't know was that he didn't *want* to be like his father.

Dale admired Julian's head for business and tried to emulate it. Not a bad thing. But Dale's word was gold. Once given, he stood by it. His father broke his word as a matter of habit. At Massey International, Dale cleaned up the consequences. He made the hard calls. His father's personal life was far messier than work. Julian fell in and out of love with the seasons. Like some men changed their wardrobes, his father changed relationships, oftentimes ignoring his sons in the process. Dale had cleaned up some of his brothers' messes, too.

Commitment was something Dale didn't offer a woman. Love couldn't exist without commitment, so Dale made sure he didn't fall in love, either. No problems so far. He hadn't earned his nickname for nothing. With a cold heart came protection.

Dale exited his room and had walked a couple of steps when he heard the music. A violin, to be exact, and it sounded beautiful. Someone liked classical music. Odd, considering the number of country radio stations he'd clicked through on the drive home.

Home?

Since when did he think of Shaw Ranch as home? Dale shook his head and muttered, "Figure of speech."

The music stopped midway through a piece. Then it started again. That wasn't a radio. That was live. Someone played the violin and Dale wanted to know who.

He stepped carefully, hearing murmurs of conversation floating up from the living room. The Shaw family gathered below to watch TV. He heard the crackle of wood burning in the big stone fireplace and could smell the warm scent of wood smoke.

The music stopped again, and he heard a feminine-sounding cough. He stood near a door left ajar that led to that violin, so he knocked.

"Just a minute." Faith's voice and then her pretty face when she opened the door, instrument in hand.

He felt as if he was slipping on ice again. "That was you?"

She nodded and opened the door wider. "Come on in. I'm practicing."

He glanced down the hallway with its wraparound balcony open to the lower level. He really didn't want her family to think he was putting the moves on her.

Faith waved away his concern. "I'll leave the door wide open, don't worry."

He followed her inside.

"Would you like something to drink? I have pop and iced tea in the fridge."

"I'm fine. Thank you."

He took in the tiny dorm fridge in the corner under a small countertop and sink. A coffeemaker and containers of coffee and tea bags were neatly nestled in a row.

"You're wearing your new jacket." She sounded pleased.

"Yes."

She lifted the violin to her shoulder. "It looks good on you."

"Thanks." He slipped out of it, draping it over the arm of a puffy couch as he continued his perusal of the space.

Faith's room was bigger than his and had the feel of a studio apartment. A very feminine studio painted in light shades of yellow and white where there were no logs or pine paneling. A wrought-iron bed with tons of pillows and an old quilt angled against the opposite corner. A wall of bifold doors hinted at a huge closet before cornering toward a bathroom. Pictures of her family and horses and the mountains plastered the walls.

He spotted another picture atop a bookcase and walked toward it. A photo of Faith and her sister dressed for an evening out. Faith wore black velvet and her hair had been styled and secured with rhinestones. Her lips smoldered dark red. He knew how soft those lips felt against his own.

"That was taken in Seattle, when I worked with a symphony there." She stood next to him.

"Lovely." An inadequate response, but all he could manage.

Dale knew beautiful women. He'd dated plenty of them. But he couldn't recall ever seeing an expression quite like the one on Faith's face in the picture. Anticipation and joy and innocence were rolled into one special look for whomever had taken the photo.

Had there been a man behind the camera lens? Envy seared him quick and sharp.

"Sit and relax for a bit." Faith used her bow to point toward the couch. "Or were you going somewhere?"

"For a walk, but I'd rather hear you play. Will that bother you?"

She smiled. "Not at all."

"Do you play around here, then?" He couldn't imagine Jasper Gulch having an orchestra, no matter how small. He made himself comfortable on the couch.

"Bozeman." She tilted her head against the instrument and studied the sheets of music on a stand in front of her. "You like the classics?"

"We've got a box at the Met and Avery Fisher Hall." He'd attended his share of operas, plays and concerts.

Faith's eyes bulged. "The New York Philharmonic?"

"That's the one." He'd finally managed to impress her. He wouldn't mind taking her to a concert and watch her eyes light up as she listened.

"Wow."

Dale chuckled.

No knuckle cracking or stretching, Faith jumped right into playing and her movements were fluid. Slim fingers slid along the strings and her arm dipped and sawed gracefully with the bow. Occasionally, she'd look up at him over the music stand and smile.

Not the same look as the one in the photo.

What would it take for Faith to look at him like that? Seriously, he needed to get out of Dodge as soon as possible.

"Okay, what's going on in here?" A very deep male voice exaggerated the harsh words.

Dale looked at Cord Shaw. "Listening to your sister play. She's good."

"Yeah?" Cord tipped his head as if he hadn't

thought about it before. "Wait till you hear her play Granddad's fiddle. Now, *that's* talent."

Dale glanced at Faith.

She rolled her eyes.

"Katie and I are taking Marci home. Thought I'd say good-night and thank you again, Dale, for coming all this way."

Dale didn't quite buy the gratitude. Someone had sent Cord up here to check on them. Dale stood and extended his hand. "You're welcome."

Cord took it in a hard grip, but his eyes turned serious before he let go. "Not too late, Faith."

"Yes, sir." She gave him a mock salute.

Dale received the message coming from Cord's eyes and strong handshake loud and clear. Treat his sister with respect or there'd be trouble. Dale had no intention of doing otherwise. "No need to worry. I'm not staying long."

Faith's brother seemed to get his meaning and nodded, satisfied.

Staying too long in Jasper Gulch had consequences. Namely, wanting more from a violin-playing beauty than he could deliver in return. Dale didn't do serious relationships. When it came right down to it, he didn't know how. And that suited him well.

After Cord had left, Faith continued to play, but her heart wasn't into it. Not with Dale watching her every move with trepidation. Did he think she'd make him pledge his soul after one kiss? She wouldn't mind if he did, but still.

Oh, why did she favor men who wouldn't want her for the long haul of forever? She sighed and swung her violin from her shoulder.

"You're done?" Dale looked disappointed.

"For now." Faith settled the wooden instrument into its case. "Are you hungry?"

Dale's eyes narrowed. "Maybe."

"There should be cookies or something good downstairs in the kitchen. Come on, before they send someone else to check on us."

He grabbed his dull red barn coat. The one that looked so good on him. "How about a walk?"

"Sure." Faith opened her closet door, grabbed a sweatshirt and slipped it over her T-shirt.

They headed downstairs. Faith leaned over the back of the sofa and petted Ranger, who sprawled on her mom's lap. "We're going for a walk."

Her mom smiled. "Be careful."

"Of course."

Dale stood silently near the foyer waiting. He looked as if he was headed for a dentist's appointment—stern faced and maybe even a little nervous.

Grabbing her coat, she asked, "You sure you want to do this?"

"Fresh air will do me some good. I need to finish up a sales report."

"Don't you ever stop working?"

He shrugged as he held the front door open for her.

"So, what is it that you do, anyway?" Faith lifted the hood of her coat and stuffed her hands into mittens.

"In a nutshell, I manage a company that buys and sells property and convinces other companies to buy and sell property."

"Oh. That really clears it up." Faith laughed. "So, your father owns it?"

"The shareholders own it. My grandfather started it, my father's the CEO and I manage the rest."

They walked down the paved driveway, the sound of their feet scuffling against the asphalt in the quiet of night. "Do your brothers work with you, too?"

His breath billowed white in the cold night air. "They're young."

Faith tipped her head. "Like in high school?"

"Eric is twenty-five. Jordan is twenty-three and just finished up his studies abroad."

"Tell me about them."

Dale shrugged. "Not much to tell. We're not that close. Eric skis all over the world, and Jordan… Well, Jordan is Jordan. A serious kid, he's worked two internships, in England and Hong Kong, respectively. He stepped into Massey International this past September."

"So Jordan takes after you."

He looked grim, as if he'd never considered that before.

Faith moved on. "Is that why we went to that ski resort?"

"Julian wants to purchase an office in a location that might lure my brother into the business fold. I think it's a bad idea."

She wrinkled her nose. "You call your father by his first name?"

Dale looked even more grim. "Sometimes."

Which Massey would get their way? If they had an office near here, maybe Dale would come back. Faith tamped down misplaced hope. Dale said he didn't ski. Why would he return to Montana? Unless she gave him a reason to…

They made it to the paddock, and Faith's horse trotted toward them and nickered. Faith rubbed the mare's nose. "This pretty lady is Viv. Short for Vivaldi."

Dale looked at her mare. "Will she bite?"

"Not if you're nice to her." Faith laughed at Dale's hesitation. "I'm kidding. Go ahead and give her a pet."

Dale stroked the middle of the mare's dark face down to the white spot at the end of her nose. Viv stepped closer to him for more of the same.

"She likes you." The man had a way with females.

Dale laughed and scratched behind Viv's ears. "How long have you been playing the violin?"

"Since I was knee high."

"Why that particular instrument?"

Faith leaned against the fence and watched Viv nuzzle Dale for more attention. "My grandfather on my mom's side played a mean fiddle. I remember Christmases where he'd play carols and we'd all sing and dance. I wanted to make that kind of magic happen, too, so he taught me. And then I took lessons."

"And learned the classics?"

Faith nodded. "Yes. I love classical music. Those notes have been around for centuries and they still have power to move the soul. I believe some of them were written as worship to God. A gift that keeps on giving to the rest of us."

He shrugged. "I suppose."

Faith tipped her head. "Don't you believe in God?"

"Yes. In a general sense I suppose I do."

"Well, God's more about up close and personal. He wants what's inside versus the outside rituals."

Dale looked as if he wasn't in the mood for a theological discussion. Or maybe it was the lack of sophistication in the topic. "Where'd you study music?"

"Montana State."

"Why not out East? Julliard or Eastman. That's where the prestigious schools are located." Dale stepped away from petting Viv.

Faith cocked her head. "I don't care about prestige. I have everything I want right here."

Not a man to call my own. And not the man standing in front of her who was sorry he'd kissed her.

Dale looked at his hand and grimaced. "Maybe we should head back."

"Why?"

He looked horrified. "Because my hands are filthy."

Faith laughed out loud. "Come on, greenhorn. I'll show you where you can wash them."

Clothes didn't make the man. No matter how many Montana barn coats Dale wore, he was no Montana man, complaining about dirty hands. He didn't belong here. But could he? If he ever belonged to her?

Chapter Six

Dale scrubbed his hands at the sink inside the spacious barn. The earthy scent of hay and leather assaulted his nose. There was something honest about it. Something simple, too. Unlike the sterile office-space air he breathed on a regular basis.

Hands dripping, he looked around for a towel.

"Sorry, you're going to have to air dry." Faith leaned against a stall and pointed at the empty paper-towel holder on the wall.

Dale shook his hands. He caught Faith giving him an odd look. "What?"

"Just wipe them on your jeans."

"I'm not going to do that."

She shook her head. "I didn't ask you to jump off a bridge."

"So, I'm a *greenhorn* and a neat one, at that. So what?" He stared at all the empty stalls. "Don't you keep your horses inside the barn?"

"It's better for them to be outside where they can stretch and run and breathe. We bring them in to saddle up and take care of their shoes, or if the weather turns bad."

Dale nodded and then his phone vibrated in his pocket. He looked at the incoming call from his father. "Excuse me. I have to take this. It'll only take a minute."

"No problem. I'll be outside."

"Dale Massey." He watched Faith slip out the door. He could see her breath make white smoke where she stood waiting for him.

"What reservations do you have on that property?" Julian asked. Never a greeting, never a how are you. Always business with his father. And that was all. *Always*.

Dale ran his hand through his hair. "Doesn't feel right."

"That place is perfect for Eric."

"You didn't see it." Dale didn't trust Eric to toe the company line. His half brother was apt to ski far more than work with an office like that. They'd waste time and money.

"I don't have to. You're my eyes. What else have you looked at?"

"I haven't." Dale never snowed his father. Julian would see right through it.

"Then what in the world are you doing out there?"

A pair of big blue eyes came to mind. "I'm staying at the mayor's ranch with obligations to my host."

Julian laughed. "So there's a woman involved. Have your bit of fun, Dale, but I expect you to snatch up that offer before—"

The call ended. Dropped.

Again.

Dale growled.

Faith peeked her head inside the open door. "Everything okay?"

"Spotty cell coverage! How do you people live here?"

Faith's eyes widened at his sharp tone, and then narrowed. "We live here just fine."

"Of course you do." He hadn't meant to insult her. He checked his watch. "Look, it's getting late and I've got work to do."

Only nine o'clock, but he was tired. In New York, he'd rarely get to bed before midnight and then he'd be back in the office by seven. Montana time was only two hours behind the eastern time zone, so jet lag wasn't an issue. Maybe all this fresh mountain air made him sleepy.

"What do you do besides work, talk and text on your cell phone, Dale Massey? What do you do for fun?" Faith stepped closer.

Simple fun? He couldn't remember. Every activity had a purpose. Entertaining clients, entertaining women, entertaining his next move as heir to Massey International. "I play tennis, remember?"

Faith shook her head. "The way you play doesn't sound fun at all."

"I play to win. Winning is fun."

She stared at him.

He stared back.

The overhead light bathed Faith in its glow, caressing her hair with shine where it wasn't covered by the knitted hat she wore. Dressed in yoga pants and bulky boots, she looked young.

Too young for someone like him.

"How old are you?"

Faith laughed. "Slick guy like you should know that's no question to ask a woman."

Her hesitation hinted that she might be older than he thought. She'd graduated college, but when? He raised his eyebrow.

"I'm twenty-seven. How old are you?"

"Thirty."

Faith clicked her tongue. "Old enough to know that all work and no play makes Dale a dull boy."

"You think I'm dull?"

She'd be the only woman to think so. His daily schedule made most people's head spin. Yet this slip of a girl made him feel incomplete. Like something was missing.

Her gaze softened. "You don't really want to know what I think."

He stepped toward her. "I do."

She gripped her mittened hands in front of her. Was that to keep from touching him?

They were close enough that one more step would bring them together. Dale slammed his hands in his pockets to keep from touching her. No way would he repeat today's kiss. They might not make it out of this barn and that wasn't Dale's style.

"Honestly, you seem a little lost to me."

He searched her eyes. What made her think that? Lost? He knew exactly where he was going. His future was laid out nice and clear in front of him. But that road suddenly looked cold and lonely.

"Lost, huh? Well, right now I'm charting my way back inside. I'm beat."

"Yeah, sure." Faith looked away. "Let's go."

What did she want from him? Whatever it was, he couldn't go there. Faith deserved a good man who would love her forever. A loyal, committed man.

That man wasn't him.

They made their way back along the driveway, walking the rest of the way in silent darkness, save for the lights shining from inside Shaw Ranch.

"Good night, Dale." Faith hesitated at the doorway of his room.

She wanted to kiss him again but knew better. He was used to women throwing themselves at him. She didn't want to be one more. How embarrassing.

"Why do you think I'm lost?"

She fixed his barn-coat collar, which had turned under. "I get the feeling that you go through the motions without passion."

His eyebrows rose and he gave her a look that challenged that statement.

She let loose a nervous giggle. "Dale…"

"I'm good at what I do." His voice sounded whisper soft.

"I'm sure you are, but is it enough?"

"Good night, Faith." His eyes dismissed her. Guarded again. Then he went inside and closed the door.

Faith stared at his closed door a few seconds before making her feet move. She headed for her own room and met her brother Adam in the hallway.

"How's loverboy?" Adam wrapped his arms around himself and made mock-kissing sounds.

Faith punched his arm. "How old are you?"

"Not much more than you." Adam laughed and scooped her up over his shoulder like a sack of grain. He trotted down the hall. "Dad wants you."

Faith bounced against his shoulder and paddled her brother's backside with both hands. "Put me down."

He laughed and kept going, ignoring her plea.

Ranger joined in the fun by jumping against Adam's legs and barking.

Faith spotted Dale coming back out of his room, looking surprised at the ruckus.

"Help!"

He smiled. "I don't interfere with family matters."

"Coward," she yelled, bouncing all the way down the stairs hanging over Adam's shoulder.

Dale followed them with an amused look on his face.

And Faith didn't want to be embarrassed. Ha! Draped over her brother's shoulder was a real nice start. "Adam, put me down. Dale might need something."

"I'm sure he does." Her brother didn't comply, though.

Their mom intervened and scooped up the dog. "Adam, put your sister down."

"Aw, Mom." Adam finally set her on her feet and gave her a shove, to boot.

Faith wobbled.

"Your father wants to talk to you about tomorrow's homecoming. I'll help Dale."

Faith glanced up at Dale, fearing her face was redder than a Christmas bow. He looked amused as he gestured for a phone. Her mom stepped in, and Dale followed her to their landline.

Faith wasn't needed and took off after Adam. She body slammed her brother into the wall and then ducked into her father's home office before Adam could retaliate.

Her father looked up. "Really, Faith?"

She giggled. "He started it."

Her father shook his head. "I'm heading to town early in the morning but want to make sure you're ready for tomorrow's event. Dale needs to be there by eleven for photos."

"Yeah, I know. Wait, why not tell him this?"

"I want you to drive him there." Her father gave her a look that brooked no argument.

"He can make it on his own, don't you think?"

Her father nodded. "You've spent a lot of time with our Mr. Massey today."

"So?" She'd followed her father's orders to cart Dale around but didn't dare let on that she'd enjoyed it.

"So? Why not give him a reason to stay for Thanksgiving? The town is counting on having a Massey in the parade, and having someone of Dale's status might be a good media draw."

Faith ignored the butterflies in her stomach. "Dale said he has business in New York."

"You can convince him to stay if you put your mind to it."

He eyes widened. "Dad!"

Her father smiled innocently. "What? You two made eyes at each other all through dinner."

"We did not!" Faith had avoided looking at Dale. She didn't want to make any big moves that might scare the man completely away after that devastating kiss.

"Weather might get dicey by midmorning. Forecast calls for freezing drizzle and I don't think Dale will be safe in that rental."

"We'll see in the morning." Faith stood.

"Think about it, Faith. He's a good match for you."

Tell her something she didn't already know. And if it was indeed true, how did she make Dale see that, too? There was something real simmering between them, but that didn't mean he'd want to stay. Didn't mean he'd want to stay with her, either.

"Good night, Dad." She kissed her father's cheek and left.

The house had quieted down early for a Friday night. Julie and Ryan had long since left for Julie's bungalow on the hill. Cord and Katie had taken Marci and gone home, too. Austin was out on a date, and even Adam had quieted down, unless he hid in waiting.

Faith entered the kitchen and found her mom by the sink. "Where's Adam?"

"He went to bed. It'll be an early morning getting the horses inside the barn before the weather hits."

Faith picked up Ranger and snuggled him close. She'd help, too. "Did you take care of Dale?"

Her mom smiled. "He needed to use the phone."

Faith glanced at the clock. After ten. Which meant

it was after midnight in New York. "Kind of late for a business call, don't you think?"

Her mother shrugged. "Oh, I don't know. Something about property in the mountain resorts, but I told Dale that he should look at buying property right here in Jasper Gulch."

"Why'd you do that?" Faith could just imagine Dale's reaction to her mother's eavesdropping on his call. He'd clench his jaw and swallow his irritation with a polite smile.

"There are whole buildings up for sale in town, and cheap, too. And so I told him."

Faith reached for a cookie from the snack plate her mother had fixed for her father. "What did he say?"

"That he'd keep it in mind." Her mom smiled.

It was a knowing smile, one that made Faith cringe for letting her hope show. Would Dale consider buying here? It would mean so much to Jasper Gulch. It would mean even more to her.

Dale woke to an odd sound. A high-pitched *ting, ting, ting* against the window. He rolled over and looked at the clock. Eight-thirty. It had been a long time since he'd slept so late. Snuggling deeper under his covers, he heard it again, only louder and more steady.

His eyes flew open and he jumped out of bed and looked outside. White balls of ice gathered at the edge of the driveway and pooled in the grass.

Sleet.

He fumbled with his laptop, entering the password Faith had given him to connect to the internet. He let loose a groan as he waited. When he finally checked the weather, it wasn't pretty. The radar map showed a mass of moisture barreling down on Montana. Globs of green were followed by a mass of pink. Behind it was snow. A forecast of bad news for the area.

Next, he checked his airline flight out of Bozeman later this evening. No changes yet, but cancellations were bound to follow once that storm hit. Unless he got there ahead of it and hopped the next plane heading east.

Dale showered and dressed quickly and then packed. He had a couple of shopping bags compliments of Miss Shaw and her hardware store. Slipping downstairs, Dale saw the house was quiet, but he didn't believe the Shaws were asleep. He'd seen lights shining from the barn and remembered what Faith had said about the horses and bad weather. No doubt they were corralling them into stalls even now.

He left his luggage in the foyer and headed for the dining room and coffee carafes set up on a sideboard. He couldn't leave without saying goodbye to Faith.

He heard the door open and the stamp of small feet. *Faith.*

Setting down his cup of coffee, he looked up as

Faith entered the room dressed for outside work in heavy canvas overalls. How long had she been up while he slumbered?

Her blue eyes wide, she asked, "Why's your luggage in the foyer?"

"Because I'm leaving."

"The homecoming is only a few hours away." The reason he'd come.

"There's a storm brewing and I need to stay ahead of it." And get out while he could.

Faith's blue eyes snapped with fury. "What am I supposed to tell my family? They're counting on you to be there. The whole town is looking forward to meeting you."

"Things change. I'm sure they'll understand."

She shook her head. "No, they won't. My father won't. We need what you bring to this gathering."

He narrowed his gaze. The real reason for Jasper Gulch's excitement wasn't his lineage to Silas but what the Massey name meant now. The name his father had put on the map would no doubt bring notoriety to their hokey little gathering. He shouldn't care. Good business was good business and everyone had an angle they played.

He downed the rest of his coffee with one gulp. "You'll have to make do without me."

"Would it be so bad to stay?" Her voice softened.

Looking at her, his resolve weakened. He couldn't

afford what a few more days spent with Faith might do to him. "Yes, it would."

Her shoulders drooped.

"Thank you for your help yesterday," he said. "Take care of yourself."

She wouldn't look at him. "You, too."

He sighed. Why'd she have to look so disappointed and hurt? "I'll show myself out."

"No, no. That would be rude. I'll walk you to the door."

"Where's the rest of your family?" He couldn't stand the awkward silence.

"Dad's already in town. The guys are checking on windbreaks for the cattle, and my mom, Katie and Marci are helping Julie herd her sheep into the small barn."

It dawned on him that Faith had taken care of the horses all alone. "I could have helped you with those horses."

She gave him a funny look.

Her hesitation said all he needed to know. He was useless out here. He'd have been more of a hindrance than help. He didn't know anything about ranch work. Like she'd said, a *greenhorn*.

He lifted his luggage and reached for his shopping bags, but Faith had them in hand, ready to follow him to his car.

He opened the door, and the damp sting of cold air bit his face. "This doesn't look good."

"No."

He followed Faith out from under the metal-roof overhang, and sleet pricked his skin and bounced off his long woolen coat. Could he stay ahead of this front? He'd planned to take another look at that property before flying out of Bozeman. That probably wasn't wise. He'd stick to the interstate and go straight to the airport.

He started the lemon to let it warm up, and then tossed his luggage and shopping bags in the back. Faith stood next to him.

"You should go inside where it's warm."

She shrugged. "I'm fine."

Of course she was. Faith was made of stern stuff. Faith belonged here with the vast Montana land that bared one's soul. He did not.

He held out his hand. A completely inadequate and awkward gesture, but it was the best he could do. "Goodbye, then."

Faith stepped closer and slipped her hand into his. Her skin was soft and rough at the same time. "Goodbye."

He didn't want to let go. Contemplating a friendlier way to part company, Dale leaned down.

But Faith stood on tiptoe and quickly kissed his cheek. She let go and moved out of reach. "Be careful."

He nodded. "Yeah."

Would it be so bad to stay? Faith's words whispered through his mind as he climbed behind the wheel and backed up.

"It'd be disastrous," he muttered.

He drove down the driveway without a problem. He'd make it if he took it easy. He checked his rear-view mirror and clenched his jaw. Faith stood outside, watching him leave. It felt like a punch in the gut to let her down, but he kept driving.

He'd almost made it to Jasper Gulch when the sleet turned to icy rain slashing across the windshield and down the windows. He cranked up the defroster and turned on his wipers, but ice still formed. He slowed down to a crawl. The surface of the road had iced over, too.

Feeling the pull of the wheels toward the ditch, Dale overcompensated. The little rental car spun like a top, finally coming to a stop in the middle of the road. The lemon's front end pointed in the direction where he'd come from.

And Shaw Ranch.

Dale shook his head at the irony.

Leaving might have been a bad idea.

Chapter Seven

Faith leaned against the door. Dale was gone. For good. And it hurt. How could that be? She'd spent two days with him. Only two.

"You okay, Faith?" Her mom must have come in the house through the laundry room. Her hair was plastered to her head and her cheeks rosy-pink from helping Julie with the sheep.

She nodded, not trusting her voice. No way would she cry. It had been only two days. Ridiculous!

"Where's Dale? Surely he can't still be sleeping."

Faith cleared her throat. "He's gone."

"Gone?"

"Airport."

Her mother's eyes went wide. "Oh, honey, I'm sorry."

Faith sidestepped her mother's comforting embrace before she lost it. "It's fine, really. I'm fine."

She made her way up the stairs toward her room

to shower and change. Tea is what she needed. A soothing hot cup of tea. Then she'd give in and sulk.

Midway up, Faith turned. "What am I going to tell Dad?"

Her mom's expression remained concerned. "Tell him what you told me. It's not like we're going to have much of a draw from outlying areas in this weather."

"I suppose you're right." Faith peeked outside.

Rain now hit the windows with icy splats, then drizzled down the pane. Her brothers were out there in this mess checking on the cattle.

By the time Faith stepped out of the shower, she heard her father's booming voice call out her name. Something was wrong if her father had come home from his office at city hall before an important Jasper Gulch event. Throwing on her thick cotton bathrobe, she bolted from her room.

"Faith Elaine?"

She hung over the railing. "What?"

Her father stood in the living room stoking a roaring fire. "Homecoming's postponed. Already got a thick coating of ice out there with no sign of stopping."

"Okay." Faith could spend the whole day in her room practicing if she wanted. She'd feed the horses come dinnertime. Until then, they were fine in the barn. "Heard from the boys?"

Her father nodded. "I'm heading out there myself."

Dale stepped close to the fire and then looked up with a grim smile. His tan coat was torn and dirty.

Faith's heart raced. "Dale."

He gave her a nod, then stared at the flames, looking like a man defeated.

"Found him in a ditch near town." Her father held his hands out to the warmth of the flames. Both of them looked cold and wet. No, Dale looked drenched.

"What happened?" She clutched the front of her robe.

Dale looked at her. "I changed my mind about leaving." Then he smiled. "The weather helped."

His eyes said something else. Something far more personal. Or maybe that was her imagination and wishful thinking.

Her father laughed and slapped Dale on the back. "Good thing your rental spun out close to Jasper Gulch, or you'd have been stuck for sure with all the roads closing up around us. They've already closed the interstate. As it was, I almost drove past you, too."

"Yes, thank you." Dale reached his hands toward the fire.

"Make yourself at home, son. This storm might be a long one." Her father looked up at her. "Where's your mother?"

Faith shrugged. "Kitchen?"

"I'm going to throw on something dry and catch up to the boys."

"Anything I can help you with, Mayor?" Dale offered.

Her father laughed again. "Thanks, but no. Can't afford to lose sight of you out there."

"Of course." Dale's lips thinned.

And Faith felt a little sorry for him. What did he think he could do, anyway?

"I'm taking a four-wheeler." Her father left in search of her mom.

Faith slipped down the stairs. Dale hadn't moved away from the fire. Was he okay? Had he hit his head or something when his car went off the road?

Standing next to him, she noticed the slight tremors that shook him, and touched his arm. "Give me that wet coat. You need to get out of those damp clothes before you freeze."

He slipped out of the expensive wool while taking in the robe she wore. "Too late, I'm already frozen."

"Very funny." Faith bundled his coat into a ball. She'd see about having it repaired and cleaned. She looked down and noticed Dale's sock-clad feet. Thin-looking socks, too. "Didn't you wear the boots you bought?"

He shook his head. "Another pair of shoes ruined. Lost, actually, in the ditch."

Dale was a city boy through and through.

Faith pushed a chair closer to the fire. "Sit and put your feet up on the hearth. I'll be right back."

He did what he was told. "Where are you going?"

"To get you something hot to drink."

Dale watched her hustle away in that fluffy blue bathrobe and her bare feet. He felt like an inadequate fool. And useless, besides. He couldn't help his host. Not that he'd have a clue what to do, being a greenhorn.

After spinning out, he'd headed back to Shaw Ranch, but the freezing rain had coated the road with ice so quickly, the little lemon wouldn't respond to taking a curve. He'd slid right off the road into a deep ditch. He'd been trying to push the car out, using a couple of fallen tree limbs as leverage, when his shoes got sucked off his feet into the mud. Good thing the mayor had come along with that beast of a vehicle.

The heat from the fire seeped into him, warming his frozen feet. His wet socks steamed. He'd never been this cold in his life.

"Here." Faith pushed a steaming mug at him. "Hot chocolate."

He could use something a whole lot stronger but sipped it anyway. "Thanks."

She bent down, stripped off his wet socks and looked ready to toss them into the flames.

"Those are cashmere." He couldn't believe they'd

stayed on, but they were well made. Good elastic construction.

"These are useless." She tossed them on the floor.

What kind of man couldn't take care of himself in the elements? But then, in New York, he'd never had to. Assistance was a phone call away with loads of cell coverage. He stared at his red toes, which were tingling with sharp needle pricks. He wiggled them and winced.

Faith looked at him with soft compassion. Like a wise woman might view the village idiot. "You're fortunate my dad came by."

"Yes." The mayor had hooked up a strap to the rental and pulled it out in no time. Jackson Shaw's truck tires had chains on them, so it was pretty easy towing the lemon back to Shaw Ranch.

"I'm going to get dressed. Do you want anything?"

He stared at Faith's pretty face that had been scrubbed clean from a shower. Her hair was wet too. Seconds ticked by before Dale finally shook his head. "The phone, maybe, but later."

She smiled.

And Dale's stomach dropped.

How long would he be trapped here?

With her.

"There goes the power," one of Faith's brothers announced.

Dale couldn't tell which one. He opened his eyes.

A blanket covered him. And a pillow had been placed under his feet.

Faith.

He swung his legs off the stone ledge of the hearth and winced when his bare feet hit the stone-tiled floor. His muscles screamed against further movement, but he ignored them and stepped forward. How long had he slept? The fire had died down some, but it still crackled and hissed. Calling him back.

He looked outside and shuddered. Fat snowflakes fell steadily, sticking to the icicles that hung from the trees and the fence and everything. Jack Frost had run amok while he was out cold.

"May I use your phone?" he asked no one in particular.

"What happened to you?" Cord asked.

"My rental went off the road."

"Dude. I've seen beat-up bullfighters that look better." Adam, the one who'd carried Faith over his shoulder, laughed.

Dale looked down. His trousers were grass-stained, blood-stained and ripped. When had he scraped his knee? His feet looked puffy and he walked as if he might be pushing seventy. "I guess the car won. Phone?"

"It's out, too. First thing to go."

Great. No phone, no power. At least his laptop

was charged. His phone, too, but that was practically useless out here. "How long will it be out?"

"Have you looked outside?" The other brother, the one who'd held his hand when they were saying grace, spoke.

Dale squinted. "Snow." It snowed in New York. He knew about snow. "So?"

All three brothers laughed.

"There's a thick coating of ice under that snow. The power's going to be out a good long while."

What did that mean? "Okay. I'm going to shower."

"That'll have to wait until we get the generator hooked up." Cord shifted his stance.

Dale wanted to bark orders to get to it, but this wasn't his home. "I'll change, then."

He heard soft notes of the violin coming from upstairs. Faith was practicing again. Something about that soothing sound only aggravated his irritation. She was good, too good to bury herself in the middle of nowhere.

Faith found God in the music. Her passion. And she was content with that find, having everything she wanted right here. He wasn't content and never had been because he could always do better, work harder and play harder, but none of that would erase his reality. He'd never been enough for his father to stay with his mom.

He made his way to the foyer and grabbed his bags. Passing by a mirror, he got a glimpse of himself and nearly laughed, too. His hair stuck straight up. He hadn't bothered to shave this morning, and his five-o'clock shadow had moved to mountain time.

Once in his room, Dale stripped out of his clothes and tossed his pants in the trash. He wanted a shower but made do with what water he could dribble into the sink. Dressed in the jeans and a warm flannel shirt Faith had picked out, he settled down with his laptop.

Connecting to the internet was impossible. Once the generator was hooked up, he'd send an email to his assistant that he'd been waylaid in Jasper Gulch by weather. He couldn't even contact the property manager at Lone Peak. An odd sense of satisfaction that he didn't have to make that purchase settled him down some.

Then he got to work, opening files sent by Jeannie and his father for review. It didn't take long to burn through his laptop charge. With a growl, he slapped the lid shut and stood.

Snow still fell outside, coming down thick and heavy. His stomach rumbled. He'd missed breakfast and lunch. He crossed the room and flicked on a light. Nothing. How long did it take to hook up a generator?

Dale exited his room. He'd talk to the mayor about this. Jackson Shaw was a man of business. He'd understand Dale's need to keeping working.

* * *

Faith felt her mouth drop open.

Dale Massey, dressed in jeans and a flannel shirt, walked into the great room and headed straight for her dad. His hair wasn't slicked back like the other day, but full and messy. And his stubble-roughened jaw made him look, well, like a bit of a cowboy. A ruggedly handsome one, too.

"Mayor, have you had a chance to hook up the generator?"

Her father glanced at her with a twinkle in his eye.

She shut her mouth.

That made her dad smile even broader. "Yes, Mr. Massey. We were able to hook up the generator."

Dale spread his hands wide. "The lights in my room don't come on and none of the outlets work."

"That's right. I've turned off breakers in the house to conserve on the gas needed to run the generator. We don't know how long the power will be out, but we're ready. We have plenty of food and water."

Dale looked relieved. "Good, I have a ton of work to do and my laptop's dead. So, if you'll point me to an outlet that does work—"

"Sorry, Dale, but I can't allow you to do that."

"Sir?"

"Like I said, we have to manage our resources and be careful of what power we use. We've got animals to care for. A short shower is fine, but I won't run down my fuel with a lot of lights and charging of electronics when heat and water is more important. I expect we'll be one of the last groups to have our power restored, considering our location."

Faith watched Dale digest this news. His neck burned red-hot. He might be good at controlling his reactions, his emotions even, but right now, it was pretty easy to guess his thoughts and they were not happy ones.

"Have you eaten anything today, Dale?"

"No, sir. Not much."

"Faith, get this man a snack, would you?" Her father snapped his newspaper back into place. Conversation over.

Faith got up. "Come on."

Dale followed silently until they were in the kitchen. "Is he serious?"

"About limiting usage? Unfortunately, yes." The power hadn't gone out like this in years, but Faith remembered having to be selective in what they used.

Dale hooked his thumb over his shoulder. "He's the mayor. Isn't he on the priority list?"

Faith stared at him. The flannel Dale wore gaped at the base of his neck exposing part of his collarbone. Even that looked strong and manly, especially without one of those stuffy undershirts. "No. The elderly come first here."

Dale ran a hand through his hair. "This is crazy. I've got work to do."

"Would it kill you to give your laptop and phone a rest?"

He gave her a sharp look. "It might."

Faith bit her tongue as she fixed Dale a sandwich. Could he be more self-centered? This weather situation was serious. "You want work to do? You can help me with the horses after you eat."

"Fine." He tore into his sandwich and then mumbled around a mouthful, "Thank you."

Faith grabbed a handful of potato chips. Munching a chip, she glanced outside. It was still snowing heavy wet snow. Might be better to keep the horses in the barn overnight. Her brothers and father had used the ATVs to check on the cattle earlier. Her brothers were out there dropping hay with the big tractor now. Hopefully, they wouldn't get stuck.

"You look worried," Dale said softly.

"That's a lot of snow piling up."

"We get snow in New York. Slows everyone down a bit, but it's not too bad. Upstate gets more, of course."

Faith looked at him. He really didn't get it. She shouldn't expect him to. "The mountains get tons of snow, and the people who live up there are used to handling it. We don't get as much here in the valley. It snows, then melts, snows a little more and some stays. This much all at once could be real trouble."

"With the return of power?"

"Keeping the cattle fed and watered and warm.

Their winter coats are in, but if it gets super cold after they've gotten wet?" Faith shrugged.

"You might lose some?" Dale looked like he finally understood the implications of that terrible possibility.

She didn't want to think about cattle losses. Her father and brothers had built up a fine herd with strong bloodlines. Those animals were tough. "We'll do what we can, and pray that we don't."

A subdued Dale placed his plate and glass in the sink and followed her to the closet in the foyer. He wore his felt-lined boots this time and the wool-lined barn coat.

Slipping into her own coat and boots, Faith handed Dale a hat and work gloves, then called out to her father. "We're going to feed and water the horses."

"Okay. Your mother's helping Julie with her sheep. Check on them while you're at it. Ryan's helping the boys."

"Will do." Faith opened the door for Dale.

He gave her a crooked grin as he walked out. "I'm supposed to do that."

"Oh, please." Faith pulled her scarf closer around her neck.

Dale chuckled. "Lead the way."

Faith tromped through the wet, heavy snow. They had about a foot on the ground already.

Once inside the barn, she stamped her feet and the horses nickered softly. "Hi, guys."

"They seem restless." Dale brushed snow from his shoulders.

"They want back outside. Come on." Faith entered their grain room and handed Dale a bucket and a big scoop. "Each horse gets a full scoop."

"Okay."

She took the lid off the grain barrel and scooped up the fragrant mix of oats with molasses. Once their buckets were full, they made the rounds. Faith stood on tiptoe to lean over the top of a stall and emptied half the scoop of grain into a corner feed trough. The horse stuck his nose into the food before she'd finished.

Dale looked hesitant.

Faith laughed as she moved to the next stall. "Don't worry. It's easy."

"If you say so." He was tall enough to lean over and dump the grain.

Her mare, Viv, spotted Dale and whinnied. Faith laughed again. "I think she has a crush on you."

"To be lowered to the level of animal appreciation."

"You've got it all wrong there." She dumped the last of her grain and returned to fill it. "Animals know more about people than people."

Dale refilled his bucket, too. "So you think."

"So I know. Viv doesn't take to just anyone. She's a rescue and whoever had her first didn't treat her kindly. There's something mighty gentle in you for her to want your attention."

Dale stopped scooping grain and looked at her, horrified, as if she'd uncovered his big secret. "Gentle, huh? I don't think my father would agree. I've made some pretty brutal deals in my day."

Faith frowned. "Don't tell me you're a cutthroat."

"I don't take overinflated values well."

"Yours or theirs?" Faith wondered if he had an ethical base he worked from. Dale might believe there was a God, but he didn't strike her as man of faith. He'd pretty much admitted to spending holidays with non-family members of the female persuasion.

"Both. Repeat business demands a level of honest negotiation and fair pricing. But I won't be taken in, and I don't have a problem cutting loose dead weight in the office."

She smiled. Viv might be on to something. Underneath the stuffy clothes and sophistication, Dale Massey might be a good man. Strong and confident, he did what needed to be done.

When they finished with the grain, Faith showed Dale the water pump, and they gave each horse a fresh water bucket. Outside, Faith cracked away the ice that had formed on the water trough in the paddock and then plugged in the deicer to keep the water from freezing.

"That's it for now. Want to see Julie's sheep?"

Dale shrugged. "Sure."

"They're sweet things."

"Why do you have sheep? I thought sheep and cattle don't mix."

Faith smiled, amazed that he knew that much. Although anyone who'd ever watched a nature special on TV probably knew that much. Both animals graze, competing for the same grass.

"Exactly right. But Julie's been raising them since she was a kid in 4-H. My dad gave her some pastureland and she's made quite a business for herself. She sells the wool and knitted creations online. Katie, Cord's wife, plans to sell some in town when she opens Jasper Gulch's first-ever boutique."

"A good tourist-shopping draw. Locally made goods."

Faith nodded. "If we ever get the tourists here."

Dale slipped into the crowded sheep barn behind Faith to the sound of feminine laughter and the bleating of sheep. Two large, hairy white dogs slept like sentinels by the door. Despite the windows, the day was dark and gray even with the snow. The women had a couple of lanterns burning.

Nadine and Katie and the young girl named Marci fawned over a lamb that followed Julie around like a dog. Another dog followed her, too, along with Nadine's poodle. Both dogs barked, but the larger one nosed the small white lamb back toward the pen.

"That's Cowboy Dan." Faith pointed.

The dog heard his name and came bounding for them. Tail wagging furiously, the long-haired spotted thing's tongue hung from his mouth. Cowboy Dan sat down in front of him.

Dale looked at Faith. "What does he want?"

She giggled. "For you to pet him."

He did his best not to make a face. Then he remembered the work gloves. Slipping them back on, he patted the dog's head.

"He won't bite you." Julie smiled.

"I'm not much of an animal guy."

Julie and Nadine exchanged looks. Animals were their livelihood.

The little lamb wandered near him, too. Or maybe it was Cowboy Dan who'd herded the creature his way.

"I don't know, Viv sure likes you." Faith scratched under the chin of one of the bigger sheep in a pen. "And now Cowboy Dan, and even the little lamb there."

Dale looked around. "There's a lot of sheep in here."

"With the icy rain, I didn't want them to get wet then cold. Their wool hasn't filled out from their fall shearing." Julie puttered around the barn, tossing hay and a different kind of grain into troughs.

It smelled earthy in here, too. Thick like molasses. And a bit dusty from the hay.

"Dad wanted me to check on you, and see if you need help." Faith still scratched the sheep that looked blissful with its eyes closed.

"We're done here." Nadine brushed her hands against her jeans. "Might as well get dinner started."

Dale watched the women file out of the smaller barn and followed. Julie remained behind.

Making their way back to the main house through the fat snowflakes, Dale considered the simplicity of life here. It was not easy by any means, but it was not the hustle and bustle of what he was used to. And certainly not the cold indifference.

Shedding his coat and boots, he stepped into the large living room with the roaring fire and women's chatter. This warm and woodsy atmosphere was light-years away from his modern co-op with the stark-metal-and-gray-leather furniture. Nothing like his mother's overly decorated condo and even his father's posh penthouse. Shaw Ranch had a welcoming feel to it. A pull on him he didn't want to examine. He didn't belong here.

Surrounded by the finest all his life, maybe he'd missed something basic. Being part of a close-knit family might be part of that, but there was something else. He wasn't sure what it was, but maybe stuck out here, he'd find it. Or better yet, he'd realize this wasn't real and lasting, either, at least not for him.

Chapter Eight

"Morning." Faith skipped into the dining room. Although the temperatures had dipped low overnight, glorious early-morning sun peeked through the dark clouds and streamed through the windows, turning the snow outside into a carpet of sparkly white cotton. The ice had become a coating of crystal.

Her parents and two brothers were already seated, their plates full of eggs. Dale was there, too. Their eyes met and held.

Faith's appetite fled, replaced by a swishy feeling. Those butterflies were acting up again, making her light-headed. She looked away. Noticed the shared smiles between her parents and kicked herself for mooning over Dale in front of them. Going after Dale Massey was a delicate operation. She didn't need her parents' obvious matchmaking efforts getting in her way.

"We're checking the fences this morning. The wind kicked up overnight and there might be drifts." Adam poured a glass of juice. "Dad's going to attempt to plow the driveway."

"Sounds good." Faith filled her plate. Plowing the wet, heavy snow from their private road and driveway before it froze into a solid mass would take her father a good portion of the morning. And Dale had said he wanted to work, so keeping her voice even and nonchalant, she asked, "Dale, would you like to go with me?"

"Sure."

Austin nodded his way. "We could use the help. Cord and Ryan are evidently sleeping in. Do you ride?"

"I do. Or rather, I have. I belonged to a polo pony club while studying in England. But it's been a while."

"I see." Austin raised his eyebrows at Faith.

She ignored it and sat next to Adam, putting her directly across from Dale. "I don't know who could sleep with all this sunshine."

"They're newlyweds," her mom said with a wink.

Faith felt her cheeks heat. "Oh, yeah."

"You ever been married, Dale?" Adam asked.

Faith kicked him under the table. What kind of a question was that?

"Ow."

"Uh, no." Dale sipped his coffee with a look of

utter distaste. Marriage wasn't the plague. But then, his parents were divorced.

"Can't say I'd ever want to. Makes a man soft." Adam leaned back in his chair. "Look at Ryan and Cord lazing about."

"As if you'd find someone who'd have you." Austin knocked his brother's shoulder.

"Marriage strengthens a man." Her father took her mother's hand and they shared a look. Something deep and filled with understanding passed between them. "With the right woman, it makes him a better person."

"Thank you, Jackson." Her mom smiled. They'd been under a lot of stress these last few months consumed with centennial preparations. Then she leaned forward and kissed him quick.

Faith wanted to slip under the table.

Her brothers made sounds of illness.

Jackson gave Dale a nod. "Might be just what you need."

Dale's green eyes widened.

Her heart skipped a beat or two and her stomach turned over. Nope, not obvious. Not at all.

"Thank you, sir, but I'm fine as I am." Dale's expression was closed. Humorless.

Austin gave her a look of sympathy and rose from the table. "We'll see you out there."

And Faith could have hugged him when that diverted their father's attention. They left, and silence thick as molasses settled in the room.

"I'll head for the kitchen." Faith's mom took the tray of dirty dishes and left. Between her volunteer work and time spent on various Jasper Gulch committees and boards, Nadine Shaw's time was usually filled. On weekends, she liked to putter around her kitchen.

"Sandy's not here," Faith said to cut the silence. "But then, today's Sunday and she has the weekends off anyway."

Dale nodded. He didn't care about their housekeeper's schedule. He looked like he didn't care about much.

She took a bite of eggs and could barely swallow. Faith pushed her plate away and sipped coffee instead.

"You'd better eat."

Faith's eyes widened. "Well, Mr. Skip-Breakfast, you're calling the kettle black."

"What's that mean anyway?" He gave her a smirky grin.

"I don't know, but you're the one who doesn't eat in the morning."

"I did today. A whole plateful. It was delicious."

"Good for you." Her positive mood had vanished with her father's meddling. And why did Dale keep looking at her?

"No word on the power?"

Faith shrugged. "With this cold snap, that ice isn't going to melt. Bad news for the linemen and us. It'll take longer, I'm sure."

With her father's decree to conserve energy, they'd switched off breakers in the basement, closed up heating vents to unused rooms and closed the doors. It was chilly inside this morning, but they'd be outside most of the day. In the cold.

Might as well get to it.

Faith wolfed down a couple of more bites and then thoroughly looked Dale over. "You're going to want some fleece-lined jeans today. And more layers under that barn coat. Adam's got a pair. I'll fetch them for you."

He nodded, looking unperturbed. "I'll get ready, then."

When she met Dale in the hallway, he'd slipped on a fancy gray turtleneck sweater under the green flannel. Made his green eyes really pop. She'd found him a warm hat and lined leather gloves and thick wool socks, too. "Here."

"Thank you."

"Meet you downstairs."

Slipping into the coat, Dale stepped into view wearing the lined jeans, his boots and barn coat. He looked ready for outside work. Was he?

That cultured voice of his made her rethink the invitation. He didn't like getting his hands dirty. And what if something went wrong? What then?

"You sure you're okay with this?" She thrust her woolen-covered feet into thick rubber-soled boots that skimmed her knees.

"I can't sit around and wait for the electricity to come back on. I'd climb the walls."

Faith nodded. "Okay, then, let's go."

They entered the barn. The stalls were empty except for Viv and H.R.—a gentle giant of a gelding her father intended for Dale. The rest of the horses were in the paddock, no doubt enjoying the cold sunshine and fresh hay. "Ever saddle up before?"

"No."

"That pony club did all that for you?"

Those vibrant green eyes hardened. "Yes."

"Well, here's your first lesson." Faith disappeared into the tack room and came back out with a couple of blankets. "We'll saddle up your mount first. Viv gets impatient if she has to wait."

Dale chuckled. "I know how she feels."

Faith decided to cut Dale some slack. A businessman stuck on a ranch with no way to conduct his business had to feel cranky. She'd seen Dale's ironclad control crack and give way to plain old irritation. She didn't mind. It made him human.

Still, it was Sunday. A day of rest. Although, not for ranchers. Power outage aside, Dale could probably use a few hours away from laptops and cell phones and sales reports. It was up to her to make sure he didn't regret this fence-checking jaunt.

She showed Dale how to clip a lead rope from the wall to the gelding's harness so he'd stand still while they saddled up. When Faith came out of the tack room with the saddle, Dale's eyes widened.

"Give me that." He reached for the heavy leather Western-style saddle. "It's bigger than you."

Faith let him take it, knowing she'd bruised his pride earlier with her crack about the pony club. "Okay, place it on the blanket."

He gave her a sardonic look. He wasn't an idiot.

"Pull the cinch strap tight." Faith watched, and then shook her head. "A little tighter."

"Seriously?"

Faith took over. Going shoulder to belly with the horse, she pulled the strap higher and H.R. groaned.

"Aren't you hurting him?" Dale stood close behind her.

Faith chuckled as she anchored the leather strap in place. "He's a sweetie but bloats his belly on purpose, hoping to be left behind to eat more hay. You've got to gently remind them who's the boss."

"I see." He made no move to step back. "What's next?"

Faith looked up, feeling her breath catch at how close they stood. "The reins."

"Show me how to do that."

Faith licked her lips. Did he really want to know or was he humoring her to pass the time? She softly elbowed him in the ribs. "Give me some room here."

He backed up.

She felt his gaze on her as she grabbed the reins from the door of the gelding's stall. The air seemed tight and charged and it sure wasn't compliments of the dead power lines trying to come back to life. Dale Massey burned holes through her.

Faith cleared her throat and looked up at him. "What?"

He cocked an eyebrow.

"You're, like, staring."

He chuckled. "I'm watching to learn."

Learn what, though, that was the question. She was pretty sure Dale wouldn't be doing this again, any time soon.

"Getting them to open their mouths is something of a dance. Rubbing the bit against their teeth usually works." She maneuvered her arm underneath H.R.'s jaw and slipped the bit into the gelding's mouth. "There's a good boy. Then loop the top over his ears, like so."

"Got it."

She smiled. "Good. Now, mount up and I'll make sure the stirrups are long enough for you."

Faith watched Dale swing into the saddle with easy grace. "Not bad."

"I haven't done anything yet."

"You got on well. That's a good start." She handed him the reins.

He looked way too good sitting in a saddle. Faith

had trouble dragging her gaze away from his rough, unshaven face. Dale Massey sort of resembled the portrait of his great-great-grandfather, Silas. And Faith had always thought Silas a handsome fellow.

"Sit tight while I saddle up Viv." She'd unhook the gelding once they were ready to go. She didn't want Dale taking off when she wasn't ready.

"I'm not going anywhere." Dale scratched behind the gelding's ears.

If only that were really true. Faith sighed. As soon as the power came back on, Dale might be gone. He'd been nothing but honest with her, sharing his code of flirting ethics and warning her that he didn't do *serious*. Dale sounded like a real player and yet, he seemed more like a man afraid to feel too much. And that made her wonder why. It also made her want to set him free.

Some wild things can't be tamed.

But Dale wasn't wild. He was the most guarded, controlled man she'd ever met. And honest. Scott had lied to her from the start, making her believe he truly cared when he hadn't.

And here she was again, chasing after love the way she'd chased butterflies as a little girl. She'd never used a net as a kid. Faith hadn't wanted to crush them by accident. After many failed attempts, she'd finally caught a beauty with her bare hands. Gently, she'd let that monarch walk her fingers right up her arm until it flew away. She'd never have experienced that special connection had she given up.

Might Dale be her monarch?

If so, she'd have to tread softly, and hope in the end that he didn't fly away.

Dale followed close behind Faith as she led the way through deep packed snow. His horse was a gentle fellow and picked his way gingerly through the packed snow. "What's his name?"

"H.R."

"H.R.?" What kind of name was that for a horse?

"Short for Home Run." Faith turned in her saddle to look at him. "He came with the name. My father bought him from Mick McGuire after his wife died. She had a soft spot for H.R. and I think the memories were too much for Mick."

"Memories have a way of doing that." Dale couldn't believe he'd said that.

Faith gave him a curious look. "I suppose they do."

No way was he going inside that opened door. "Why didn't you stay in Seattle?"

Her eyes widened and then she shrugged. "I wasn't interested in selling my soul for a permanent seat in the strings section."

"What does that mean?"

"I dated my mentor." She scrunched up her nose, as if embarrassed to go on.

"And?"

"A big mistake. But since I'm a country bumpkin who didn't know any better, I thought he actually cared for me."

Dale knew where this was going and his gut burned. He realized who'd taken the picture of Faith dressed in black velvet. That guy was scum. "I'm sorry."

Again, she shrugged. "Don't be. I suppose I needed a lesson in growing up. He used his position and the women he mentored. I refused to be used, so I left. Seattle is light-years away from Jasper Gulch and not everyone there is worth trusting."

"So you came home."

Faith patted Viv's shoulder, and the horse swished her tail in response. "Like a whipped pup. But after a while, I realized what I had right here. The symphony I play for in Bozeman is about sharing the sheer joy of music. It's not about egos or prestige. We're a tight-knit group who look out for each other and fill in for each other. I won't find that in a big-city ensemble."

Dale tamped down the urge to strangle the guy who'd hurt her. "You're talented. Don't you ever wonder how far you could go?"

She tipped her head. "To what purpose? There are a zillion violinists all clamoring for a seat in the larger orchestras. Anyone can go there and do that. Only I can bring what I have to Bozeman. I'm needed there. Striving to improve isn't all about me but about the difference I can make. I hope to mentor students when I'm more seasoned. Maybe one day I'll get there."

"You will." Who was he to give her advice?

He'd worked his whole life to be the best, but it didn't quite satisfy him. She sounded as if she had it all figured out.

"God willing, I will. There's a Psalm that says, *Delight yourself in the Lord, and He will give you the desires of your heart.* So it's really all about Him anyway."

"You seem to know the Bible." The girl tossed out scripture the way he referenced interest rates.

She shrugged and her cheeks turned pink. "We used to memorize verses in Sunday school, and well, some of them stuck and sure come in handy. But I read the Good Book daily. What about you? Have you ever read it before?"

"In boarding school, I took a class on religion. So I've read some of the Bible, but it was awkward with all those thees and thous."

"There's a more modern translation in the drawer of your nightstand. With the power out, if you're looking to get your hands on some paperwork, pop it open. You might be surprised by what you read." She winked at him.

Dale was pretty sure he'd never been winked at by a woman who quoted scripture. "Yeah, maybe."

That admission brought another wide smile to Faith's pretty mouth. She cared for more than the bottom line and top dollar and certainly didn't need magazine articles written about her talents to know her own worth. Faith Shaw had nothing to prove to anyone. Surrounded by love and acceptance, the woman had strength of character.

Not to mention the redheaded dynamo was physically strong. And lovely sitting in the saddle with that hair flaming in the sunshine.

Her cheeks blushed. "What?"

He'd been staring. "You're different than any woman I've ever met."

"Is that good or bad?"

"Very good." He smiled. "But maybe bad, too."

Her eyes widened. "Why?"

Why indeed. He looked around. "Aren't we supposed to be looking at the fence line?"

They'd wandered away from it a bit.

"I've been looking."

He hadn't. Dale couldn't seem to keep his eyes or his thoughts off her.

H.R. took that moment to shake—his whole body.

"Is he okay?" Dale stayed in the saddle fine but wasn't sure if the horse would lie down on him.

"He's fine. He doesn't get ridden as much as he should."

Dale patted H.R.'s back, near his blond mane. "He's a nice horse."

"You two look good together." Faith giggled.

"Thanks." Dale breathed in the crisp air and looked around. Despite the frigid temperature, the sun actually warmed his back, so he wasn't the least bit cold.

The surrounding land was vast and covered in white. Straw-colored tall grass poked up through the snow in places, especially against the long, long line of wire fence they were supposed to be checking.

Dale scanned the flat pastureland surrounded by distant mountains with purple tops. All of it capped with a big blue sky. He might as well be a speck of dust compared to that huge expanse of big sky. *Big Sky.* Maybe that's how the area had gotten its name.

"How much land does your family own?"

"Couple of thousand acres or so. I'm not real sure. Dad bought up some recently."

Untapped potential, all this land. "So folks are selling?"

"Are you kidding? Land is gold out here, and not many sell if they don't have to. But times are tough, and jobs are scarce in Jasper Gulch, so yeah, some folks are selling. Are you looking at buying?"

Dale laughed, but he didn't miss the glint in her eyes. "I'm a New York boy."

"I forgot that for a moment." Her smile faltered.

So had he. "What exactly are we looking for on the fence?"

Faith shook her head. "Breaches, or downed

fence line and posts, or high drifts of snow. Anyplace where the cattle might get out. And we'd better cover more ground. See those clouds?"

"Yeah?"

"More snow's on the way."

"Oh." He hadn't noticed the change in weather. He'd been too busy watching her.

"Yep, you are a New York boy." Faith sounded disappointed.

What did she expect? Playing cowboy might be fun for a bit, but he had a job to do and a life to return to in New York.

After a long day in the saddle and a hearty meal of chili and corn bread, Dale was ready for bed. But Nadine wouldn't hear of it. She gathered her kids and *him* around the fireplace for cookies and hot chocolate. He didn't bother to ask how much generator energy it took to bake those cookies when they melted in his mouth.

When he was growing up, homemade chocolate chip cookies were scarce in the Massey household. His mom had been too worried about her weight and had banned all things sweet from their condo. Even at boarding school, cookies were rationed like silver. And Nadine's tasted better than the ones he bought in New York, at the deli around the corner. He reached for another.

Faith's sister, Julie, and her husband sat on the

floor by the fire playing checkers. The couple seemed as if they were in a world of their own, communicating with long looks and soft touches. He supposed that's what it was like to be in love. Knowing each other so well that words weren't necessary.

Faith's brothers each sank into leather chairs while he sat with Nadine and the mayor on the other couch. Oil lanterns had been lit in the living room as they'd been in the dining room.

"More romantic than battery-powered lights," Nadine had said.

Faith had rolled her eyes.

He glanced where she sat at a small table in the corner close to the fire with her nose buried in a puzzle by the light of a battery-powered camping lantern. Who did puzzles?

"This reminds me of Christmas, with all of us together like this with nowhere to go." Nadine sighed.

"Looks like it, too," Adam said. "Outside, anyway."

Dale glanced out the windows at the blizzard-like conditions. Snow fell sideways and the wind howled. How much more would fall atop the foot and a half that was already out there? He had a bad feeling that power restoration anytime soon might be wishful thinking.

"'Silent night, holy night...'" Nadine sang softly.

Adam joined in with a rich-sounding baritone. "'All is calm. All is bright.'"

Soon the whole family joined in song.

Dale listened, oddly moved by the unity this family displayed. They worked together, lived close to each other and enjoyed time spent together. They loved each other.

"Faith, get your fiddle." He'd never heard the mayor speak so softly.

She grinned and ran for the stairs.

Nadine turned to him. "My father's fiddle. He first taught Faith how to play when she was little."

Dale nodded. Faith had told him about that the other day. Seemed like aeons ago.

Faith played the instrument as she descended the stairs with a spring to her step. It was a lively tune that sounded very different from the classics he'd heard her play before. When she hit the main floor, she sort of skipped to the music, looking young and vibrant.

"'Go tell it on the mountain. Over the hills and everywhere. Go tell it on the mountain that Jesus Christ is born…'"

The Shaws sang, Nadine clapped and Dale heard a couple of foot stomps, but he watched Faith move as she played, unable to look away. The fiddle she cradled was a lighter wood color than the rich tones of her violin. Worn in places, it looked older, too. An antique that would no doubt bring big bucks at auction back East.

Not that Faith would ever sell her grandfather's

fiddle. Her family's history meant too much to her. That was the kind of woman she was, finding more value than the worth in dollars and cents.

What was it like to have that kind of connection to relatives and the past? To a town? Dale had never really known his grandfather, Silas Massey's grandson. He had an aunt who lived upstate that he rarely saw. Family gatherings like this one with the Shaws didn't happen for the Masseys.

Dale soaked in the singing. He listened because he didn't know the words. He didn't understand the closed eyes or the heartfelt nodding. Sure, he tapped his foot, but something else was going on here. Something deeper and almost reverent.

God was in the music.

When the song finally ended, no one spoke right away. A hush had settled over this family. Why?

"I think we need to pray." The mayor looked moved. Like a man battling bad memories, Jackson Shaw had deep lines etched between his eyebrows. He leaned forward and rested his elbows on his knees. "Since the weather kept us home on a Sunday morn, I think we need to thank the good Lord for His provision, His protection, and above all else, His salvation. We don't always get it right, but He loves us anyway. Amen."

Amens echoed around the room.

Dale nodded. He wasn't a religious man, but he believed in honesty, and this had that and then some written all over it. He glanced at Faith, who looked at him and smiled.

She played another tune and no one sang this time. Closing her eyes, Faith delivered a haunting melody that sounded old but not anything like the classical scores he'd heard her play. He responded to this music, feeling moved by a tug of something he couldn't name.

Too soon, Faith finished the tune, opened her eyes, grinned and launched into a jaunty version of "Jingle Bells." More foot stomping and singing. This time Dale joined in. He knew the words.

Faith noticed and gave him a wide smile.

It blistered through him with a different kind of heat than he was used to. More radiant than simply a physical response, he felt that warmth down deep in his heart. *Dale the Coldheart* might be melting. The others in the room seemed to fade into the background. He barely heard their voices as he focused on her.

Faith Shaw was like an answer to a prayer he'd never said aloud. But that couldn't be. Dale had never been a praying man. He saw no reason to start now.

Chapter Nine

"Right here, it goes right here." Faith took the puzzle piece from Dale's fingers and snapped it in place. "See?"

"I see." His voice sounded soft.

They were the only two who hadn't left early for their beds, and silence had settled over the living room, save for the soft crackle of the fire. Snow continued to fall outside and the house had grown chilly.

Faith wrapped the long cardigan knit by Julie a little tighter around her and ignored the soul-searching look Dale gave her, had been giving her all night. She scanned the table for red puzzle pieces. She wanted to complete the cactus flower before moving into the sky. The puzzle depicted an Arizona landscape at sunset.

"So you like puzzles?" Dale tried to jam another wrong piece into place.

Faith took that one away from him, too. "I love them."

He sat back with a defeated sigh. "This is a waste of time."

"It's relaxing."

He shook his head. "It's frustrating."

Faith laughed. "Not when you get the hang of it. We usually have a puzzle going through the holidays. It's a nice way to connect with each other instead of sitting like a bunch of lumps watching TV. Although the boys like being lumps."

Dale chuckled. "Your family does a lot together."

Faith detected a hint of envy in his voice. "We do. Especially at Christmas. We cut down a tree together, decorate it, sing some carols like tonight, you know, the whole shebang."

"The whole shebang." He sounded as if he didn't know at all what she meant.

"I'm sure some of that might change now that Cord and Katie have Marci to look out for and Julie's married. They'll have families of their own with new traditions to start."

"And you like tradition."

"Sure do." She turned a puzzle piece around and it fit. "Are there any Massey-family traditions?"

Dale didn't answer right away.

She watched as he carelessly grabbed a puzzle piece and found its home by accident. "Hey, look. You got one."

He gave her a grim smile. "One."

She laughed as she rose and tossed another couple of logs on the low fire. The wood caught quickly, throwing off delicious heat with a symphony of snaps and pops.

Faith returned to their table but didn't sit down. She stared at the puzzle pieces neatly grouped by color and then checked the boxed picture of the finished product. She needed perspective before moving into pieces of sky.

Dale found another piece of blue sky that he fit into place. "Top that, puzzle-girl."

"I'm pretty sure I already have." Faith started filling in the opposite-side bottom corner of sand and scrub, having long since completed the exterior frame of the picture. She'd let Dale have the sky, even though he didn't have the patience for it.

"You like to compete, don't you?"

Dale shrugged. "It's my nature, I guess. But then, I couldn't do what I do without a competitive edge."

She nodded.

After a few moments of silently working on their respective parts of the puzzle, Faith asked what had bothered her ever since Dale had said it. "Why do you go away for the holidays?"

Dale grabbed a couple of more blue pieces. "My father's been married several times, but I'm the product of his first marriage. When I was growing up, Christmases blurred into the same routine as I was chauffeured between two homes, my mom's and my dad's. Some years my father wasn't even there. Me and my half brothers were showered with expensive gifts, but there'd never been much thought behind them. It was just stuff.

"Julian's wife of the moment tried to entertain us as best she could, but what did she care about boys who didn't belong to her? By the time I'd hit college, I stopped going home for Christmas. That's my tradition."

Faith's heart twisted. How sad. "I'm so sorry."

He chuckled. "Don't be. Warm sand and sun does wonders for a person."

She didn't buy his bravado. "For spring break, maybe, but not Christmas."

He shrugged.

Faith dug deeper. "And that's why you don't believe in marriage, either, isn't it?"

He looked at her. "My father left my mother on Christmas Day when I was six. Out of the blue, he told her he'd met someone else. My mom used me as leverage, telling my father I was his duty to stay."

Faith sucked in her breath. Who'd want to be anyone's duty? "What happened?"

"He looked at me and still walked out the door."

Her heart broke when she saw the pain in Dale's eyes. A grown man, but inside those green eyes of his, she saw a little boy's rejection. Ebenezer Scrooge came to mind and how that character had been left behind at school for every Christmas holiday. Would Dale also turn into a bitter man with a wound so deep that it had never healed? Without learning to love and be loved in return?

And how could Dale work so closely with the man who'd inflicted such a wound? Unless being the best was Dale's way of proving he was more than a man's duty. As the heir of Massey International, did Dale hope to show his father that he was worth loving?

She tamped down the desire to pull him into her arms right then. Dale Massey was worth far more than he believed. But any attempt to show him would come off as shallow sympathy or worse.

So Faith didn't say anything but handed him a blue puzzle piece.

He pushed it into a piece of top border. Not a fit. He turned it around and still a no go. "Marriages don't last, and I refuse to do that to a kid."

Faith nodded. No sense in pointing out that some marriages did last. Especially those grounded in faith and reliance on God.

"What about you?"

Faith leaned back and thought about it. "Other than the obvious reason, I like coming and going as I please. I'm not ready to settle down."

But she might be, with the right man.

Dale tipped his head as he studied her. "What obvious reason?"

"The right man hasn't come along and asked."

"Their loss." Again with that smooth, lady-killer smile of his that hid so much.

"Thanks, but maybe more so my gain."

"True."

Dale might be that *right man,* but then she might be chasing after pipe dreams and butterflies. They didn't share the same beliefs or values. He'd return to New York as soon as he could and bury himself in his fancy phone and sales reports. The man might be a workaholic but he didn't like his hands dirty. Dale Massey was the furthest thing from her idea of the *right man.*

Until he'd kissed her.

After several attempts to make a blue-sky piece of the puzzle fit, he finally tossed it aside. "I'm done."

"The sky is the hardest part. All the pieces look the same."

He rubbed his forehead. "My eyes are crossing."

"You do look tired."

"Tired was hours ago. I might be heading for delirious." He stood and stretched.

Faith laughed. "Good night, Dale."

He gave her a tender smile that made Faith's heart race. "Good night, Faith. And thanks."

"For what?"

"I've never told anyone why I don't do Christmas. Thanks for listening."

"Sure." She watched him walk away.

Talking might ease Dale's hurt, but only God

could heal the wound he carried. If Dale opened his heart.

Faith tossed her puzzle piece aside and stared at the flames dancing in the hearth. She didn't want Dale ending up like some modern-day Scrooge. He had warmth and a gentleness of spirit despite the arrogance he hid behind.

And like the story of *A Christmas Carol,* Faith wanted Dale to experience the joy of Christmas before he left. Help him understand the reason for the holiday and why he couldn't give it up, not yet. There had to be a way to show him. But how?

Dale woke up to weak light streaming through the windows. What time was it? He glanced at the digital clock that remained black. Power had not been restored. He cringed when he thought about what he'd missed, cut off from the world like this.

He checked his watch, threw the covers back and swung out of bed. His muscles protested fast movement. A day in the saddle had definitely left its mark. He stretched, and grabbed his phone that still had some juice, gingerly wandering the room until he had the most bars flickering in and out. He hit the button for his assistant.

"Massey International," Jeannie said.

He got through!

"Jeannie, power's out, and I'm not sure when I can make it out of here."

"No need to rush home, Dale. I rescheduled your closings for the Monday following Thanksgiving. One of the buyers couldn't make it anyway."

She'd bought him time. "You're amazing."

"Remember this come review time…" Her voice faded out.

"Jeannie?" He checked his screen. Dropped! Again.

With a sigh he peeked out the window. Snow fell softly as if they were inside one of those glass globes. He could see the Shaw men heading out with more bales of hay for the cattle. How many cattle did they have? The plowed driveway looked icy in spots where it wasn't packed with snow.

Ice hung from the barn roof, the fences, the house. How far along was the power company? He still had to get out of here. He ran a hand through his hair, surprised at the hollow feeling that came with the thought of leaving.

He didn't belong here. Even Silas had skipped town way back when. Dale's family connections were weak and surface level at best. He might rule supreme in his eighteenth-floor office overlooking Central Park, but that's where his legacy began and ended. It's all he had. He needed to get back to it before he actually believed it possible to have more.

Dale sat on the bed and looked at the nightstand. Opening the drawer, he spotted the Bible that lay there. It was a thick paperback that didn't look near as intimidating as the tome he'd tried to read at school.

He picked it up and thumbed through the pages. He remembered reading parts of the Bible. The beginning chapters depicting creation, and he recognized the word *Corinthians*. He'd read those pages before.

Starting at 2 Corinthians, chapter 1, Dale read a brief summary about the upcoming group of letters from the apostle Paul. Helpful, that little bit of reference. The explained theme of triumph over adversity caught his eye, so he read on. And on.

After several chapters of reading in plain modern English, Dale was impressed. Paul was a man of his word. And he had sound advice to impart, although Dale didn't quite understand all of it. One particular verse stood out, stating that God would welcome him and be his Father.

Interesting concept. That God could be more than God?

Dale closed the book. Maybe he'd read more later.

He took a quick shower under warm water and grimaced when his feet hit a chilly floor. The mayor had adjusted the hot-water tank to conserve energy. No matter how far Dale turned the hot-water knob, the water warmed only so far. Maddening. Were the roads passable today? The mayor had cleared the Shaws' private road that led toward town. Surely power would follow soon.

By the time Dale entered the dining room, he was sure he'd missed breakfast. But seated at the table was Faith, munching on something that looked good.

"Hey." He poured himself a cup of coffee.

Faith's smile was bright as sunshine. "Morning. I've got a great idea if you're up for it."

He couldn't help smiling back. "What's that?"

"Would you be willing to ride into the woods with me to cut down a Christmas tree?"

He furrowed his brow. Was this *idea* the result of what he'd admitted last night? "Isn't it a little early?"

Faith shrugged. "A little, but since we're pretty much stuck here without power, my family's all in one place for once. The centennial celebrations have kept everyone busy. Tonight might be the only opportunity for us to decorate together as a family."

He wasn't part of her family, but looking into Faith's big blue eyes, he couldn't refuse her. "Sure, why not."

"Morning, Dale." Nadine entered with a plate of steaming muffins. "Hot out of the oven, if you'd like one, they're zucchini walnut. There's also an egg-scramble casserole in the chafing dish."

"Thanks." Dale grabbed a muffin with a napkin. He'd eat more, though. He'd learned to look forward to breakfast since arriving in Montana.

"Faith, I brought the tree stand down from the attic."

"Thanks, Mom."

Nadine smiled at him. "We have some beautiful trees behind the hill where Julie and Ryan live. With the guys busy dropping more hay, I'm glad you're here to help Faith bring a tree home."

"Should be a novel experience." He'd never cut down a Christmas tree before. Massey trees had always been artificial and professionally decorated. Even the office tree in the lobby was decked out by a designer.

"I hope so." Nadine sat down and helped herself to a muffin and coffee. "I'm heading into town with your father to assess the damage of the ice storm. When the power comes on, we'll have to work in homecoming before the Thanksgiving dinner and parade. All the hors d'oeuvres have been prepped and frozen. With the power out, they'll thaw and won't keep much longer. This will be a balancing act for sure, but nothing we can't handle."

Faith nodded and then looked at him with a question in her eyes.

With his closings rescheduled, there was no reason not to stay. Homecoming was the reason he'd come. That and the office space opportunity at Lone Peak, but he'd made his decision on that, too. He didn't even know if Bozeman had been hit with ice or if the airport was open again.

He looked at Faith and smiled. "I suppose I'm stuck here for a while yet."

Faith smiled back.

So did Nadine. In fact, Faith's mom looked very pleased with this turn of events. "Good. Cord went into town to assess the progress on getting power back. We'll know more today."

Until then, he might as well enjoy his Christmas-tree search. With Faith it'd be an adventure. Funny, but he looked forward to it.

Faith held out her hand to catch a few fat snow-flakes on her glove. It had warmed up some, but they'd still get a couple of more inches by nightfall according to the weather report on the radio in the barn. They'd both listened while saddling up the horses. North of Jasper Gulch had been hit hard by ice, Bozeman included. Dale wasn't going anywhere anytime soon.

She kept her eye on Dale riding H.R. as they care-fully picked their way up the hill near Julie's bun-galow. H.R. was a big but sure-footed horse, and he responded well to Dale even in snow. Dale didn't look like a city slicker today. He looked good in the saddle. A far cry from that stuffy man wearing that awful olive-colored suit.

That had been only a few days ago, and yet Dale seemed different. Somehow softer and more relaxed. Faith smiled, glad she'd let her mom in on her plan to give Dale Christmas before he left Jasper Gulch.

And that pinch to her heart whenever she thought of Dale leaving? *That* she ignored, because she hoped he might stay. She wanted to be the reason he'd stay.

"How far?"

Faith urged Viv forward, so she rode ahead of Dale while they slowly trekked downhill. "See that valley of pines? We'll find one there."

Dale shook his head.

"What?"

"Your family has so much land. And the views here are amazing."

Faith grinned. "I know. Would you like to see mine?"

"Yours?"

"My chunk of land where I hope to build someday."

Dale looked hesitant.

"Come on. It's on the other side of this valley. I've even got my own little fork of the creek that runs across the pasture and empties into our little lake. Cord's house is on the other side there." Maybe she chattered too much, but she really wanted Dale to see her land. Like a test of sorts, his reaction to it was key. For her.

Faith clicked her tongue for Viv to move forward through the valley of pines, across the creek, and then Faith reined in to a stop. "This is it."

Dale leaned forward in his saddle and looked around.

Faith watched Dale.

The land had a gentle slope and lay tucked between a rise of hills and the pine forest they'd ridden through. Not too far from the ranch, with easy access for a future road, but far enough away to feel secluded.

"Well, what do you think?"

"Nice."

"Just nice? Look at that view of the mountains beyond the pasture. In the summer this meadow is littered with wildflowers and see, there's the little stream. I think there might even be a natural spring. I'll put my house right beside it and maybe even dig out a pond."

Instead of following where she pointed, he looked at her.

She stopped talking.

"This spot suits you," Dale finally said.

"Yeah? How so?" Curious. Would it suit him, too? What would a city guy like him do way out here? Learn to relax for one.

He laughed. "I don't know. Any minute I expect the Seven Dwarfs to come marching around the corner."

She laughed, too. And then asked, "You're the real estate guru, what kind of house would you build?"

He looked thoughtful. "Log and stone are nice, but I'd go modern with lots of glass. Maybe with a slanted roof toward the back to protect against wind and give the snow someplace to slide. Make it look like the house grew out of that rise."

"Yes. I'd like the house to blend into, but not overpower, the landscape." Faith loved his insight.

Those visions of him here came back with a vengeance. It was so easy to dream about building that house together. Oh, for pity's sake! Why couldn't he see it, too?

Patience. She really needed to practice a little patience.

Faith cleared her throat. "Let's get that tree."

"Lead the way."

She turned her mare and they headed back the way they'd come. Halfway into the thickest growth of evergreens, she slipped off Viv and loosely tied her reins to the branch of a spruce.

Dale did the same. "Will they be okay like this?"

She chuckled. "They'll be fine. We won't go far."

Silently, they tromped through the calf-deep snow where it hadn't drifted deeper. Straw-colored grass poked through around and in between trees. The air smelled fresh of pine sap and cedar and snow.

Faith broke off a small cedar branch and breathed deep. "Smells like Christmas."

Dale chuckled when she handed it to him, but he sniffed it, too. "Nice."

He wasn't nearly as talkative today as last night. Maybe he was humoring her. Knowing he was stuck here, maybe he figured he might as well go along for the ride. Did he mind passing the time watching her make a fool of herself with all that talk about her future dream house? He did watch her a lot, though, almost as if considering…

Her heart pumped a little harder. That was nothing more than wishful thinking on her part or maybe plain old attraction on his. Nothing to get excited about.

Faith stopped and looked around. "I don't know, but I feel we're getting close. A lot more smaller trees here."

"You call these small?" Dale looked up.

"The tree goes up in the living room. Lots of clearance with a vaulted ceiling—we can easily bring back an eight-or nine-footer."

Dale looked around and then pointed. "What about that one?"

"Pretty, but not very full. Let's remember it and then come back if we need to."

"How on earth are we going to remember where it is?"

Faith pulled some tall dry grasses up by the roots. Then she twined them together and tied the grass like a ribbon on the branch. She turned. "Like that, see?"

"Nice."

"Is that all you can say?"

"How about, let's get a tree and be done with it." His breath billowed white in front of him.

Faith frowned. Was he cold and miserable or a

lost cause where Christmas was concerned? She did this for him and wanted him to enjoy it. "The fun is in the search for the right one—a tree that wants to be this year's Christmas tree."

He gave her an amused look. "And how do you know that?"

Faith laughed. "I just do."

"You sure you weren't found under a leaf in the woods as a baby? Or maybe you're an elf dropped from Santa's sleigh." His green eyes teased.

Faith grinned. Now, *that* was getting into the spirit of things. "I don't have pointy ears."

"You're sure about that." Dale stepped closer and lifted the flap of her hat.

She looked up at him. So tall and rugged with his whiskered jaw. What had they been talking about?

Dale's cell phone rang, shattering the moment.

"Are you kidding me?" He pulled the offensive thing out of his pocket and held it to his ear as he stepped away. "Dale Massey."

Faith watched as Dale's face hardened.

"You're going to have to tell him," Dale said, and then listened. "Eric, you might want to think this through before accepting that job." He looked at her. "I'm not sure when I'll be back. In fact, why don't you and Jordan fly out here for Thanksgiving. We can talk more about it. This town actually made a float for us to ride in their parade."

Faith's heart leaped. Watching Dale smile as he

talked to his brother gave her serious hope. The man had lightened up. And he was staying for Thanksgiving, giving her at least three more days with him. Time enough to show him what they had, and what they could be.

"I'm losing you." Dale shook his phone and growled. "I can't believe I'm in the middle of nowhere and *this* is where I get a decent signal and then my phone dies."

"Everything okay?"

Dale shook his head. "My brother Eric is a dope."

His half brother had been the reason for Dale's meeting at Lone Peak to purchase an office. "Not interested in working at a ski resort?"

Dale looked disgusted. "Not interested in working. And certainly not for Massey International. After Christmas, he wants to ski across Europe with a group of friends as a field tester for some ski-equipment company. Calling that a job is a joke. It's playtime."

"Sometimes playing is good."

He squinted at her. "Not when there's work to be done, like now, finding a Christmas tree."

"That's not work."

"It's not play, either." But his eyes looked too merry for her to believe him.

"Shows you what *you* know!" She smiled.

Dale ducked down and scooped up a handful of snow. He rolled it around in his work-gloved hands. "*This* is play."

Faith backed up. "Don't even think about it."

Dale launched the snowball.

Too late, Faith turned and it hit her in the back. She scooped up snow and made a ball of her own. She threw it at Dale, who hid behind a tree and pelted her with another.

It hit her shoulder. "No fair."

Dale laughed and launched another snowball before she'd had a chance to make her second one.

So she ran toward him and shook the tree he stood behind, sending globs of snow all over him.

"Faith!" he roared.

She laughed and then squealed when he charged.

Faith took off through the trees hounded by Dale. She spotted the horses, still tied and looking bored, their backs already covered in white. They'd leave soon. As soon as they found a tree. As soon as she got one more snowball in.

Creeping as quietly as she could, snowball in hand, Faith stalked Dale. Pretty easy. She could hear him a mile away. She slipped through a line of firs, ready to pounce, but no Dale.

"Aha!" He jumped from behind her.

She squealed again, started to run but tripped and fell face-first into a small drift of snow. *"Oooff."*

She sat up, wiping her cheeks, sputtering but laughing.

Dale laughed, too. He knelt down and brushed snow from her hat. Then he took off his gloves and gently pulled chunks of snow from her hair. "You're a mess."

Faith looked into a pair of tender eyes that softened his teasing words and warmed her from the inside out. "Thanks."

Dale tipped up her chin. "Your nose is red."

Faith sniffed hard. "Probably running, too."

She slipped off her gloves and fished in her pocket for a tissue but couldn't find one. *Great.*

"Here. One of last year's Christmas gifts that I happened to stuff in my pocket before we left the ranch." He handed her a supersoft handkerchief embroidered on the corner with the letters *D* and *M.* Not a cheap bandanna like the ones her brothers carried.

She looked at him, afraid to blow her nose into something so fine. Who carried these anymore? "You sure?"

"Don't be silly. Use it."

Faith wiped her nose as delicately as she could under Dale's scrutiny.

"Better?"

She nodded. Should she hand it back or what? She tucked it into her pocket instead. "I'll wash this for you."

Dale stood and offered his hand. "I'm not worried about it."

"Well, that's good." Faith took it and stood. Considering that Dale didn't like his hands dirty, Faith was glad he didn't have a phobia or something about germs, too.

"You can keep it if you want to." Instead of letting go, Dale drew her closer.

"As a token of your favor?"

Dale chuckled. "I think it's the other way around. You're supposed to give me something." His green eyes darkened with intent as he leaned close. "And your nose is still red."

"Yours would be, too, if you fell on your face in the snow," she managed to whisper.

"Cute, too." He was so close that his lips were mere inches from hers.

Faith's heart stopped beating. She couldn't quite breathe evenly, either.

He rubbed his nose against hers. "Feels cold."

"Yeah…" Faith couldn't think with him this close. She swayed a little.

His hands gripped her waist. Steadying her. Inching even closer.

Faith looked up into his eyes and shuddered with anticipation. He was definitely going to kiss her! Would their second kiss prove as potent as the first? She aimed to find out.

Faith closed her eyes and melted the minute Dale's lips touched hers. Gentle at first, Dale didn't disappoint. Seconds ticked into blissful oblivion as he deepened the kiss and Faith returned the favor.

There was no surprise this time. No shocked

realization of a connection. Only confirmation of how deeply that connection had twined the last few days.

And then, too quickly, the kiss ended.

Dale had ended it.

"What's wrong?" She nearly yanked his head back down for a repeat performance.

He smiled, but his gaze was behind her. "I think we found our tree."

Faith turned around and gasped.

The perfect tree, a young Douglas fir, stood regally tall and nicely shaped. All eight or nine feet of it. Little pinecones littered the snow, probably blown off by last night's wind.

"Did you bring an ax or something to cut it down?"

"I have a bow saw. Stay where you are and I'll fetch the horses."

He nodded.

She hesitated. Should they talk about that kiss and what it meant? Dale wasn't apologizing this time and neither would she. Faith wasn't a bit sorry. She was glad. Ecstatic.

And definitely falling head over heels.

Chapter Ten

"Here, let me." Dale took the saw from Faith's glove-covered hands. He could do this.

Scoping their towering Christmas tree, Dale thought he'd spoken too soon. What did he know about cutting down a tree? What did he know about using a saw? He looked at Faith. "Where should I cut?"

"At the base." She pointed. Her nose was still red and her lips swollen from their kiss. And more tempting than ever.

He knelt in the snow. His knees were already wet and cold. The rest of him simmered. Kissing Faith again complicated things. She offered promises he couldn't accept. Promises he'd never thought he'd wanted. What if he kissed her a third time, and a maybe a fourth?

He sawed the trunk of the tree with vigor. A heady, citrusy smell mixed with pine wafted up his nose, erasing the memory of Faith's soft scent. If he worked hard enough, maybe he'd shake these odd notions that in Faith's embrace lay his future. Holding her felt too much like coming home. But he'd never had a real home, so how could he be sure what he'd felt was real and not some snow-day fantasy?

He'd made it through the trunk in no time and the tree listed to one side. Faith pushed it over as he completed sawing the last little bit.

"Now what?" He stood and handed her the saw.

She slipped it into a leather case that hung from her saddle and then pulled rope from the same satchel. "We'll tie it up and Viv will pull it."

Dale watched as Faith went to work with the rope.

Then she looked up at him, eyes shining. "It's the perfect tree."

"I think so." The snow slowed to a few wispy flakes. "So, we're heading back, right?"

"Yep." Faith walked toward Viv. "Hand me the two ends of that rope."

Dale did as she asked, pulling the tree a little bit with each step. Faith's horse backed up and went sideways. "Has she ever done this before?"

Faith soothed Viv with sweet talk and well-placed pats. "She has, but we'll have to walk a bit until she gets used to it."

Faith tied those loose ends of rope on to metal rings on either side of the saddle all while talking softly to her horse. The woman had a way with her animal. The dark brown-colored Viv twitched her ears as if listening to Faith's instructions, then tossed her head in a nodding motion.

"I think she understands you."

Faith smiled. "Of course she does."

Dale stepped forward holding H.R.'s reins, ready for the long walk ahead. His horse whinnied and bobbed his head as if scolding him for goofing around. Dale couldn't remember the last time he'd *played* in the snow.

Especially with a woman like Faith.

They should talk about that kiss. Dale needed to set the record straight before Faith got any ideas, but the words seemed stuck in his throat. He wasn't sorry. He didn't want to ruin the next few days they had together with reasons why they'd never work. He'd simply be careful, keep things light and easy and enjoy this.

By the time they reached Shaw Ranch, Faith's brothers were also returning from dropping bales of hay for the cattle.

"What have you got there, Faith?" Austin pushed back his cowboy hat.

"Our Christmas tree."

"Little early, don't you think? We haven't even had Thanksgiving yet."

Faith shrugged. "Mom and I thought since we're all together, why not now."

Adam glanced at him. "Power's been restored in town but not the outlying areas yet. Should be soon though."

"Great. I think I'll head into town, check out your library and charge my phone and laptop. Get some work done." Dale needed to occupy his mind with more than Faith and her Christmas tree-hunting skills. He needed to reschedule his flight out of Bozeman back to New York, unless his brothers came with the corporate jet. He'd check on that, too.

She looked at him with wide blue eyes. "Take my car, okay?"

"Sure." Dale shifted in the saddle.

He'd spun out with the rental, so taking Faith's car wasn't a bad idea. But why would she sound so panicked? Didn't she think he could handle the lemon in snow? Or was she worried that he might keep driving and leave? That might have been the case a couple of days ago, but not now.

Still, sticking around a woman who wasn't the temporary kind begged for trouble. But he'd invited his brothers here, hoping Eric might change his mind about Europe if he saw the opportunities in Lone Peak. "There's an extra set of keys with my name on them hanging in the foyer. I can take care of H.R. if you want to go now."

He looked at her. Maybe she wanted him out of her hair for a while, too. Some space to get her bearings. "What about the tree?"

Faith nodded. "The boys will help me. Go on."

He slipped from the saddle. "I'll be back in a few hours, then."

"In time to decorate the tree?" She held the reins of both horses, looking completely at ease.

Dale smiled. "I wouldn't miss it."

Funny thing, too. He meant it.

Downtown Jasper Gulch was pretty quiet when Dale pulled into the library parking lot. He heard church bells chime the top of the hour. Icicles hung from the snow-covered roof. The Jasper Gulch library looked more like someone's house than a public building, but the sign said otherwise.

He got out of Faith's car and glanced at the piles of snow that had been plowed into tidy snowbanks. Once inside, Dale looked around for a computer area.

"Can I help you?"

Dale spotted a woman with a severe expression that matched the tight swirl of hair at the back of her head. He gave her a polite nod. "Do you have an area where I might charge my cell phone and laptop?"

The woman gave him a bright smile that softened her face. She held out both hands to him. "You must be Dale Massey. Welcome to Jasper Gulch."

"I am and thanks, Miss...?" He shook one of her hands, surprised by the strength of the woman's grip.

"Chauncey Hardman." She laughed.

"How did you know who I am?"

"Word gets around in a town this small. Besides, you look a little like old Silas." She winked at him.

Dale nearly laughed. Another wink. Maybe it was a Montana thing. "Portrait in the bank's safe-deposit-box room?"

The librarian laughed again, a deep hearty sound. "Oh, no. I've seen pictures my family had and I've heard stories from my grandmother. Silas was somewhat of a rascal with the ladies, but then he settled down when he married. Nearly tore the town apart when he left."

He knew Silas had married a Montana woman named Grace and that's all his father knew, too. Silas had managed to stay married to Grace until he died. Julian said that his great-great-grandmother had outlived Silas by only a year. Dale had verified the obituaries online.

"Do you have a town-history section? I'd like to learn more about my ancestors."

This time Chauncey Hardman snorted. "Not anymore. All the Jasper Gulch specific information was given over to Olivia Franklin for the homecoming event. Mostly newspaper clippings and old photos, but that'll all go into the museum."

"Museum?"

"Jasper Gulch has built a historical museum with plans to open at the end of December when we bury a new time capsule."

Faith had mentioned something about a time capsule before. This whole town really got into it.

"We turned over all we had. Between the new museum-building fund and the bridge-restoration fund, there's not much left in the coffers for additional library donations, if you know what I mean. My grandmother had a few photos, but I gave them up, too."

Jasper Gulch was laying the groundwork for tourist growth by embracing their past and displaying it. The homecoming event might prove interesting, to see those old newspaper clippings and photos, if nothing else. Nadine had said they'd work that event in before Thanksgiving. He hoped so.

Dale nodded. "I guess I'll have to wait for homecoming then. Now, if you could direct me to a plug and a place to work?"

"We do have a Montana travel section that has area history about mining and all. Even the talc mines over by Dillon are represented here."

Tempting information, but Dale needed to catch up before he spent time looking up stuff for fun. "I've got a few things to do yet."

Chauncey gave him another wink. "You take your time."

Dale nearly laughed. Was everyone in this town always so nice? "Thank you."

It didn't take long for his laptop to fire up once plugged in and partially charged. New emails swamped his in-box, along with reports, copies of building appraisals and meeting invitations.

An itinerary email caught his eye, so he opened it. Jeannie had forwarded the corporate jet's reserved flight for Jordan and Eric, arriving in Bozeman on Thursday morning. A note at the bottom came from Julian, newly returned from Hong Kong and interested in seeing the property at Lone Peak. A kernel of irritation dug deep. His father didn't trust Dale's instincts for not jumping on the office space.

Dale shook it off. The reality was that his father planned to join his sons for Thanksgiving Day. Had Jordan set this up after talking to Eric? Didn't matter. His family was coming to Jasper Gulch.

Did wonders never cease?

"Let's get this monster in the stand." Jackson Shaw slipped on his work gloves.

"The needles are pretty soft, Dad." Faith didn't think he needed gloves.

"Can't stand the sticky sap."

Faith laughed. That reminded her of something Dale might say. She stepped back and watched her father and brothers lift the tall Christmas tree into a heavy cast-iron stand. The tree listed far to one side. "Careful!"

Austin flashed an irritated look. "Just stay back out of the way."

Faith made a face and headed for the kitchen

to fill a pitcher of sugar water for the tree. If she wanted it to remain fresh through Christmas, she'd need to keep it well watered.

Returning to the living room with filled pitcher in hand, Faith breathed in the delicious scent of the fir tree. Perfectly shaped, yet not *too* perfect like a lot-trimmed tree, this one was wild and fresh. Dale's tree stood tall and proud, like him. And it smelled like Christmas.

She scraped her bottom lip with her teeth, reliving the kiss they'd shared at the foot of this tree in a flash of memory. It had felt like Christmas, searching for the right tree with a man who was wrong for her in so many ways.

Her father took off his gloves. "Your brothers said Dale went with you to get this today."

Faith nodded. Her brothers had already scattered. Both of them gone before she could enlist their help in gathering the boxes of ornaments from the basement. "He picked it out."

Her father's smile broadened. "Did he now?"

Faith felt her face flush. She knew that look. She didn't need her father's help with Dale. "Don't get any ideas, Daddy. Dale's leaving."

Again, her heart pinched at the thought, only sharper this time.

"Your mother said he's staying for Thanksgiving because of you."

Faith wanted to believe that. She'd heard him ask

his brothers to come, too, but that wasn't her news to share. It might not even happen. "Not much of a choice, considering the weather."

Dale had been sent to represent the Massey family as well as check out commercial property. Staying for Thanksgiving had everything to do with her and, hopefully, the connection they'd forged. But Dale wasn't sold on belonging here and he certainly hadn't shared how he felt about her. As much as she wanted to believe he cared, he might not. She might still be *safe* in his book, and that's what made this endeavor to win his heart so scary. What if in the end there was nothing to win?

Scott had swept her off her feet, promising things he'd had no intention of delivering. Naive as she was, she'd believed him. Dale was different. He had to be. She hoped their ending was, too. She pulled out the tangle of lights from the only box she'd grabbed from the storage closet. This alone would keep her busy for a bit. There had to be a dozen strings balled up like a rat's nest.

"You can plug those in and see if they work before hanging them."

Faith looked at her father. "What about conserving energy?"

Her father shrugged. "Doesn't matter now. With town restored, we'll be back up soon. Besides, purpose served. We got Dale off that computer of his, didn't we?"

Faith narrowed her eyes. "What do you mean?"

"How can he spend time with you if he's holed up in his room working? I shut off the breakers to that side of the house with good reason."

She felt the blood rush from her face. "You lied to him? To me?"

Her father put up his hands in defense. "Now, Faith, cutting back on electricity helps conserve gas for the generators. Who knew how much we'd need and for how long?"

Faith shook her head at her father's backpedaling. He had a habit of manipulating circumstances to get what he wanted. Something he'd been doing a lot of with the centennial celebrations, but this went too far.

Jackson Shaw might not be able to influence the weather, but that ice storm sure played right into her father's hands. It delayed Dale's departure. And gave her more than enough time to care for him.

Faith plugged in the glob of lights. They worked. Hopefully, they'd still work once she'd sorted them out into single strands. "Will you please let Dale Massey decide on his own if he wants to spend time with me? I don't need your help."

She wasn't stupid. She and Dale had something more than mere attraction going on, but that didn't mean he'd give up his life back East for her. She wouldn't give up her life here, either. Like that monarch butterfly, Dale's heart might not want to be kept.

"I don't know, honey. I've seen the way he looks at you. I say it's poetic justice, too. After what Silas Massey did to the Shaws, marrying into their money might bring some of it back."

Faith's mouth dropped as she looked at her father. She didn't care about Dale's money. "That's a horrible thing to say!"

Her father stood tall and proud, holding his sap-stained leather gloves. His expression changed to something dark and almost ruthless. "I'll tell you what's horrible. Something this town doesn't even know. Silas Massey wiped out the bank before heading for New York. He stole from an entire town without so much as looking back. No remorse. Now, *that's* horrible. If it hadn't been for Ezra Shaw shoring up the bank with his own capital, there wouldn't *be* a Jasper Gulch."

"How do you know all this?" Faith stared at her father.

"From my grandfather. Ezra had told him with a challenge to make something of this town."

"So that's why Silas left," Faith whispered.

It was so obvious, so rotten and terribly disappointing. Her girlish imaginings of Silas as a heroic gold miner crumbled.

Her father's eyes glazed over as if remembering as if it was yesterday. "Pretty much."

"That was ninety years ago."

Her father's eyes hardened. "Some things aren't meant to be forgotten. My grandfather taught me that. Made me promise—" He took a deep breath and puffed up his chest. "We Shaws are due payback."

Faith wanted no part of that kind of *payback*. "None of that has anything to do with Dale. I wouldn't care if he didn't have a dime to his name, I'd—"

She stopped right there.

Her father tilted his head. "You'd what? Love him anyway? Takes more than that to live on."

Faith closed her eyes as shame washed through her. She knew it took a common faith, and hope, but love was the greatest of these. It made all things possible. Love might open Dale's heart to God.

Her father had really crossed the line trying to force something between her and Dale. Was she doing the same thing?

Faith tossed the lights down. "I'm not having this conversation. I'm going to get the decorations."

"He'd be the perfect man for you, Faith. Think about that." Her father's voice carried.

She headed for the storage closet, more shaken than she wanted to admit. Her father had brought Dale to stay at Shaw Ranch because of an age-old family vendetta. Along with trying to marry her off. Again. Couldn't he give her any credit that she could handle her love life on her own?

Faith shook her head. What mattered to her father was Dale's money, and that made her sick. She didn't want his money. Dale was worth so much more than that.

"Hey." The man of her thoughts stood in the foyer.

Faith sucked in a breath and skidded to a halt on the tile floor. Had he heard any of that? She could barely look him in the eyes. "Hi."

Dale set down his laptop case and stepped closer. "You look troubled."

Faith nodded around the sudden lump in her throat.

"Come here." He gently pulled her into his arms.

Tempting, but all she needed was her father seeing them locked together. Bracing her hands on Dale's chest, she resisted. "Please don't."

"Let me help you get the decorations, then." Dale gave her a crooked grin.

Faith gasped. "How'd you know that?"

"I overheard you."

She narrowed her eyes. "How much did you hear?"

Dale rested his hands on her shoulders. "Enough. Let's get those decorations."

Faith nodded but her stomach dropped somewhere near her toes. She couldn't read his expression, couldn't tell whether he was angry or amused.

What could he possibly be thinking of her father? Of her?

With Dale on her heels, they walked down the steps to the lower level and she opened the door to the storage closet. "Everything's in here."

Dale looked around. "Nice and neat storage."

Faith pointed to a row of bins marked *Christmas* on the shelves. "We need all those."

"That's a lot of decorations." Dale stood with his hands on his hips, taking in the magnitude of their task.

"We have a big tree."

He smiled at her. A warm smile that brought back what had happened between them in front of that tree. "That we do."

"Dale—" She had to clear the air, tell him she didn't know what her father was up to, but would he believe her?

"So Silas Massey was a thief." He'd spoken the same time as she.

Faith's knees gave out and she sat on the step stool. "You heard everything, didn't you?"

Dale nodded. "Sorry."

"I should be apologizing to you. Dale, my father's got a lot of nerve. I'm so sorry, I had no idea—"

Dale laughed. "No worries."

Faith tipped her head, trying to read the man in front of her, but his expression was closed. A polite facade of iron control like when he'd first arrived. "How can you say that?"

He shrugged. "I'm used to it."

She felt sick all over again. Dale was used to folks going after his money. Treating him differently because of it. Faith meant what she'd said. She didn't care about the Massey fortune, she cared about the man. How could she make Dale believe that deep down in his heart?

"It all makes sense now."

Dread skittered up her spine. "What does?"

"I wondered why Silas left Jasper Gulch and picked New York. I guess that's the farthest place to run and easiest city to get lost in and hide. Especially with a stolen fortune that he wisely sunk into real estate."

Faith considered this. "My father could have it all wrong."

"Maybe. Maybe not."

"Well, yeah, but it could be something else, too. They were both miners, maybe he'd jumped Ezra's claim."

"If he ripped off the bank and left a fledgling town to fend for itself, that's pretty rotten and cowardly."

"It was ninety years ago." Faith watched him closely. Why was Dale getting so worked up over this?

"Doesn't matter. The Massey men have a history

of walking out on their responsibilities." Dale's voice had thickened.

He took this personally, as if Silas's actions had set the stage for Dale's own father's betrayal. Life didn't work like that, did it?

Faith remembered reading a scripture in the Old Testament that spoke of God not leaving the guilty unpunished, visiting iniquity on the third and fourth generations. But she also knew scripture that stated the son would not die for his father's sin. Which was it here, maybe a little of both?

Regardless, Faith didn't want Dale jumping to assumptions. "We don't even know if the story's true."

He gently tucked her hair behind her ear. "I have a feeling your buddy Rusty might know."

True. Rusty was old enough to remember the scuttle and then some. "And what if it is? What then?"

Dale looked serious but shrugged as he grabbed a bin. "I don't know, but I need to find out the truth, don't you think?"

"You can't rewrite history." Faith stacked one plastic bin atop another and lifted both.

Dale took her top bin. He already had two. "No, but I can do something about the future."

Faith almost dropped her bin. What did he mean by that? "What are you going to do?"

"I'm not sure."

Faith swallowed hard, experiencing for the first time the power of the Massey name that

Dale wielded. What did she know about this man, really? Would he use his power to benefit Jasper Gulch or would his good intentions hurt her town further?

Chapter Eleven

"Come on, come on. Let's decorate this tree." Nadine herded her adult kids into the living room after dinner.

Christmas music played from a stereo system that Dale guessed had been put in when the house was built. An instrumental version of "Jingle Bells" surrounded him. He liked Faith's version better.

Faith...

He believed her. She wasn't in on her father's machinations. She'd been genuinely upset by the mayor's words. He'd heard the whole thing, clear as day. It didn't mean he liked knowing what his great-great-grandfather had done, nor how the mayor wanted to use him for revenge. Did Jackson really think he could get his hands on the Massey millions by marrying off his daughter?

A tray of cookies had been placed on the coffee table, not that he had room to eat one after dinner.

The tree he and Faith had brought home stood to the left of the fireplace. Faith's monument of Christmas.

The power had come back on during dinner and everyone had cheered. But not Faith. She looked disappointed. He had to own he had enjoyed the novelty of the power outage, but he'd been out of the loop long enough. Glad for the time spent at the library to reconnect with Massey International, he still had work to do. Later, though. Not now. He didn't want to miss this decorating of their tree.

"You, too, Dale." Nadine patted his shoulder. "You can help string the lights."

He looked around the room where the rest of the men were lounging on leather chairs and sofas, clicking through the channels on the flat-screen TV that hung above the fireplace mantel. The women tore open plastic tubs to uncover the treasures stashed within.

The mayor tended the fire with another log or two. So different than Julian, and yet much the same. Both men threw their influence around. Jackson was used to ruling the roost, and Jasper Gulch, for that matter. The mayor saw him as a means to an end, just as Julian did. At least Jackson had a fierce love for his family. Dale had heard the mayor profess that love to his wife and kids. Julian had never uttered such words. Not to him.

Dale had always been a commodity. A good product that served Massey International well. And now the mayor wanted him for Faith because it would right some long-ago wrong. Poetic justice, he'd said. What about his daughter's happiness? Did the mayor even consider that?

Dale glanced at Faith.

She hadn't been her usual perky self during dinner. He'd known his share of women who'd been after him for more than his money. Prestige and social position, for instance. Again, Faith didn't care about those, either. She'd grown up insulated in the comfort provided by her father's ample provision, but seemed oblivious to it all.

Like many musicians, she didn't think about her surroundings in terms of dollars and cents. Faith's finer things in life were the intangibles. Things money *couldn't* buy, like honoring her grandfather's memory with the fiddle, working together on a puzzle or finding a Christmas tree. *Things* Dale had never experienced growing up.

She laughed at something her sister said as they plugged in a string of round, colored lights.

"Here, girls, you're going to need this." The mayor unfolded a stepladder and placed it near the tree.

"I'll get the top." Dale stepped forward. Faith couldn't reach that even with the ladder.

She handed him the female end of the lights. "Make sure you tuck that somewhere easy to reach so we can plug in the star. We do that last."

"Will do." He tried to catch her eye as he accepted

the task, but Faith wouldn't look at him. She'd avoided his gaze all evening. No doubt she was ashamed of what her father had said. Dale didn't want that, either. He wanted the chatterbox back.

Once the glowing lights were wrapped around and layered into the tree branches, the rest of the family got into the act of hanging ornaments. Dale sat this one out. He didn't have a bin with his name on it.

Each member of the Shaw family hung ornaments they'd either made or been given from the time they were kids. Even Cord's wife and the young girl named Marci, along with Julie's husband, had each been given an ornament as new members of the family.

"I bought them right after last month's wedding," Nadine explained as she passed out the ornaments.

Another tradition.

Faith loved tradition. He could easily picture her with kids of her own. She'd tell them stories about their Shaw history and the town's founding. Then she'd play the fiddle for them and they'd dance around their Christmas tree singing carols. A charming scene. Like something from a movie.

She finally glanced at him.

He stared back.

Faith smiled and returned to the business of decorating. Her movements were quick and sure. Ducking under the long arms of her brothers, she didn't waste time placing her ornaments. She was the first one done.

By the time the decorations were on the tree and fussed over by Nadine, who'd rearranged them several times, Dale had downed a few cookies. And a glass of milk, compliments of Faith.

He'd miss this after he left Shaw Ranch. And this family atmosphere wasn't his thing at all. In New York, he kept a pretty tight schedule. He got up, read the paper, checked the stock-market news and interest rates and then headed for work. Weekends typically consisted of more work, tennis at the club with friends, and a date or attendance at a dinner party. Dale glanced at the mayor, who sat in a leather recliner with his tablet, a deep furrow between his eyebrows. If Jackson was checking his email, he didn't care for what he read, if that frown was any indication.

"Trouble, sir?" Dale couldn't help baiting the man a bit.

The mayor gave him a shrewd look. "Nothing that can't be fixed. One of the floats has a flat tire. You know how that is, now, don't you?"

Dale didn't miss the reminder of fixing Faith's flat tire. The man had challenged him back. "Now that I know how to do that, maybe I can help."

The mayor set aside the electronic device and shook his head. "No need. Already taken care of."

Why did he get the feeling that wasn't the issue

at all? That maybe the mayor had made that one up? For what reason?

"Are you ready?" Faith brought him the star.

Dale would never willingly admit it, but his heart pumped a little harder at being given the honor. "You want me to do it?"

She nodded. "You found the tree."

He'd found something else, too. Something he wasn't ready for. Something he'd never be ready for.

Dale looked around the room. Nadine's smile was a little too broad for comfort. The mayor had looked up, too. He wore a smug expression Dale wanted to wipe away. The others waited for his acceptance to place the star on top of the tree.

It was only a Christmas decoration.

He took the star from Faith's hands, careful not to look into those big blue eyes of hers. He might not come back out.

Climbing up the stepladder, Dale jammed the rhinestone-encrusted gold star securely into place. He plugged it in and the star's white lights shone brightly. Someone turned out the lamps and the family *oohed* and *aahed*. This was more than simply plugging in a Christmas decoration. He felt like he was part of something bigger—a family tradition.

He climbed down from the ladder, folded the thing up and leaned it against a wall. Then he turned and stared at the fully decorated tree with its cheesy gold star that actually looked rather regal up there.

Despite the mismatched ornaments, the tree looked nice. Nothing like the fancy Christmas trees he was used to with tiny white lights and crystal. This was a real family tree.

His first *real* Christmas tree cut down by his own hands. He couldn't shake the satisfaction in that.

Faith stepped near him. "Well?"

He draped his arm around her shoulders. "Looks good, doesn't it?"

"I think so." She rested her head against him and slumped as if a burden had been lifted. Did she think he'd hold what her father had said against her?

He wanted to chase away all the Shaws and kiss her again. And again. Find out how real these feelings he had for her were. But he knew better. There'd be no casting himself as the lead role in that movie of Faith's future Christmases. Having a home and family to call his own tugged at his core like a fleeting wish upon a star. But the thing about movies, and Christmas movies in particular, was that they were fiction. They weren't real.

He gave her a little squeeze and then let go. "Thank you."

"You're welcome." Her voice came out soft and sweet.

She pulled out of his grasp to help the women gather up the mess of storage-bin lids and tissue paper. He made a move to help her take them back downstairs, but Katie and Julie beat him to it. Good thing, too. He'd be wise to slow down when it came to Faith Shaw. There were things he needed to be sure of and things he needed to take care of before he left Jasper Gulch. The last thing he wanted to do to Faith Shaw was hurt her.

"Do you mind if I ride into town with you?" Dale had dressed in dark gray trousers and a turtleneck sweater that probably cost more than two of her orchestra paychecks. He wore his Montana boots, as he liked to call them. Smart man.

Faith felt casual in her best jeans and a pretty, blue sweater hand-knit by Julie over a simple white T-shirt. She planned to help set up tables for tonight, so comfort was a must. "I'm not coming back before homecoming," she explained.

He smiled. "I know. I've got some things to take care of in town. I'd like to check out that new museum the librarian told me about. I'll meet you at the high school."

Faith nodded and bit back the question on her tongue. The museum wasn't open yet, so what else did he plan to do with his time before homecoming? Maybe track down Rusty Zidek? That was harmless enough.

She frowned. Why did she think Dale might do otherwise? Maybe because there was something different between them. Dale seemed almost wary of her. Did she have her father's matchmaking attempts to thank for that, or something else? Dale had been holed up in his room working all morning and then again after lunch.

"Did you get your work done?" She slipped into her coat.

Dale wound her scarf loosely around her neck. "I did."

She looked up at his clean-shaven face. She missed the whiskers. She'd miss him. He'd leave with his family after Thanksgiving and it hurt to think of him gone.

"What?" Dale tipped his head.

"Nothing." Faith looked away before she begged him to stay.

Dale gathered the collar of her jacket and pulled her closer. "What's the matter, Faith?"

She forced a smile. "Not a thing."

He searched her eyes and leaned toward her.

Faith lifted her chin in response. Kissing him would make saying goodbye that much harder, but she could no more refuse his touch than forget her name.

"You guys heading out?" Julie's voice rang out before she turned the corner. "Oh! Sorry."

Faith backed away from Dale. "Ah, yeah. I'll see you there."

Julie glanced at Dale.

"He's got business in town," Faith explained.

Her sister's eyes widened. "Oh?" When Dale didn't offer up any information, Julie kept going. "Well, setup should be a snap. I think Mom and the

Decorating Committee have been busy transforming the school cafeteria since lunchtime."

Faith slipped outside after her sister, and Dale followed them silently.

No more kisses.

Not yet.

Faith needed to regroup and plan her next attack to scale the walls Dale kept in place around his heart. As she drove into town, Dale was preoccupied with his phone. Texting or something. Whatever it was, his fingers flew across the screen.

"You finally got coverage."

He chuckled. "It's a pretty weak signal, but I'm getting what I need."

"Oh." Faith wondered what that was but didn't ask. Really, it was none of her business and Dale wasn't offering up any clues.

She finally pulled onto Main Street. "Where should I drop you off?"

"The corner is fine. I'm going to pop into the bank." Dale slipped his phone back into his pocket.

"Really?" Faith raised her eyebrows.

"Really." He grinned at her, but again offered no explanation.

She pulled up to the Great Gulch Grub café. "Here you go."

Dale stared at the restaurant's sign. "Is that for real?"

"Yes, and before you make fun of the name, the food is awesome. Everything's homemade."

"Of course it is." He leaned close, gave her a whisper of a kiss and then smiled. "See you in a few at the high school."

Faith sat stunned, watching him cross the street and head for the bank. She ran her fingers over her lips. What was that all about? A sign that he cared? Of course he did, but how deeply?

A sudden knock on the car hood startled her. Lilibeth Shoemaker shouldered her large handbag and waved.

Faith pressed the switch to open her window. "Hey."

"Are you headed for the high school?"

"I am."

"Can I catch a ride? I'm supposed to help set up." Lilibeth rolled her eyes.

It was only a few blocks, but then Lilibeth wore impossible shoes. "Sure, hop in."

The nineteen-year-old slipped into the passenger seat and her purse tipped over.

Faith noticed a stack of papers rubber banded together and glanced at Lilibeth. No sense pretending she didn't see anything. "That's a lot of paper."

The girl scooped up her handbag and settled it in her lap. "Financial-aid paperwork."

"For college?"

Lilibeth tossed her blond hair. "I've got plans. Dreams, even. Some of us aren't lucky enough to catch a multimillionaire."

Faith opened her mouth to deny catching anyone.

Not yet, anyway. But then, Lilibeth might have seen Dale's sweet little goodbye kiss when he got out of the car. Not that it meant anything. Dale had business in New York. He was leaving, and he hadn't given her any indication he was ever coming back.

Exiting of the bank, Dale spotted Cord Shaw and waved him down. "Do you have a minute?"

Faith's brother looked at him closely. "Let's go to city hall. There's a meeting room there."

"I'd rather not run into the mayor," Dale said.

Cord nodded. "Understood."

Dale followed Cord across the street and they entered the building through a side door. He'd put the guy's hackles up, but Cord appeared to be a man Dale could trust. And Faith's brother might give him straight answers.

Once inside a small conference room, Cord didn't sit down. He didn't mince words, either. "Okay, what's this all about? Faith?"

"No."

Cord stared hard. "Don't mess with my sister and break her heart. She trusts too easily."

Dale appreciated that. "I have nothing but respect for Faith."

"Uh-huh." Cord mulled that over.

Dale wasn't sure Cord believed him. "Look, I like your sister and wouldn't for the world hurt her—"

"But?" Cord looked as if he might tear him apart.

Dale chuckled. Jackson Shaw wasn't nearly as protective, but then there was that little thing about wanting the Massey money. "But I'm not here to talk about Faith. And you're going to have to trust that your sister is a smart woman."

That's all he'd say.

Cord's scrutiny weighed heavy a moment, and then, finally, the guy sighed. "Okay, I got ya. So, what did you want to know?"

"That bridge on River Road. What's the situation?"

Cord gestured toward a chair. "Have a seat."

Dale sat down, but Faith's brother exited the room.

He came back with a fat folder and tossed it on the table in front of him. "Engineer inspections, estimates and everything the council has tried to do to raise the funds to rebuild the bridge. We're far from close and, of course, my dad's done little to help with this project. When the time capsule was found by the bridge, I think some folks took it as a silent message to leave things be."

"Faith said your father doesn't want the bridge reopened."

Cord nodded. "I'm not sure why. Maybe he thinks the tragic legend of Lucy Shaw's body never being found after her car went over the side is more of a tourist draw than an opened bridge. Or like a bunch of folks here, he likes things to stay the way they are. Regardless, our town needs to grow and my dad knows that."

Dale nodded as he fingered through the papers. "Mind if I borrow these for a day or two?"

Cord's gaze narrowed. "My mom told me that your family is flying in for the Thanksgiving celebration, that you'd asked if they could stay at the ranch. If you don't mind my asking, what changed everyone's tune?"

"I used the Massey float as added incentive."

Cord laughed. "Faith will like that."

Dale nodded. He'd been in a hurry to leave since arriving, and now? Now, he had a few ideas he wanted to investigate. More time with Faith was a bonus. One he hoped neither would regret.

"Take your time with those."

"Thanks." Dale had been given approval for more than simply taking a file.

"And with Faith, too. She's a good girl." Cord's protective expression had returned.

Dale nodded. "I know. Another thing—I wanted to ask about this museum…"

The Jasper Gulch Homecoming was like no event Dale had ever attended. This was small-town America in all its glory. Red, white and blue streamers hung in an attempt to transform the high school cafeteria into a festive dining hall. Pretty tough to do with Jasper Gulch Bobcat team banners and sports records high on the walls. It still looked like a school cafeteria despite the round tables with white tablecloths and floral centerpieces sporting picks that read "100 years."

He'd done his duty by posing for several pictures to commemorate the event. He shook hands with the senator and various county officials. Confirming that he was the only Massey in attendance got old real quick, but at least more were on the way. Standing beside the Shaws for all those photos hammered home the nail. For now, he was alone.

As hors d'oeuvres were laid out, Dale wandered the perimeter of the room. Dozens of easels had been set up with old photos and newspaper articles depicting Jasper Gulch throughout those one hundred years.

Faith was busy helping Nadine and doing her duty as the mayor's daughter, but she'd given him a wave when he arrived. For now, Dale was on his own. The only Massey among scores of Shaws.

He stared at the first large poster displaying photos of the town's founding. He recognized Silas Massey from the bank's portrait, as well as Ezra Shaw. Both posed with women who had to be their wives.

Dale studied the picture closer. Grace Massey was a small woman and sort of plain. Not the type he'd imagine having the power to keep a reported ladies' man at home. Did Silas stay home? Especially after they'd arrived in New York with a fortune in hand?

"That there's Silas and his young wife, Grace." An elderly index finger, gnarled with age, pointed to a picture.

Dale turned toward Rusty Zidek. "Yes. I recognized him from the portrait hanging in the bank."

"Doesn't your family have any pictures? Be interesting to see some after they'd moved to New York."

Dale nearly laughed. The Massey photo albums were sketchy at best and more consumed with the founding and subsequent growth of Massey International. But then, he'd never asked his dad much about Silas and Grace. Or even his own grandfather. Maybe there existed old records or things he'd never been shown. "Not that I know of."

Rusty fingered his long gray mustache. "Too bad. Too many folks lose sight of their heritage these days."

"When I get back to New York, I'll see what I can find."

Rusty zeroed in on him. "That'd be real good. I'm sure the museum would be interested in copies."

Dale got straight to the point. "Did Silas really steal from the bank he helped establish?"

Rusty didn't look a bit surprised by the question. "Staying out at Shaw Ranch, I suppose you'd hear sooner or later. Jackson keeps that tight in his craw. My father knew all about the Shaw promise to keep

Silas's actions secret for the sake of the town, but venom like that leaks out on occasion."

Dale's stomach turned. "So it's true."

Rusty nodded. "I remember my pa talking about it. He helped Ezra cover up the theft to keep the bank afloat."

"Nice." Dale's heritage comprised thieves and cheaters.

Rusty narrowed his gaze with sympathy. "You can't pick your family, son."

"No, I suppose not." It didn't sit well that the Massey fortune had started with stolen money. Neither did Rusty's ability to see how much the information bothered him.

"There's a bigger family you can be part of, though. Can't guarantee it ain't equally messed up, but with it comes a whole lotta love and belonging."

"Are you talking about Jasper Gulch?" Dale chuckled. He supposed the townspeople were a family of sorts.

"God's family. His body of believers, you know, the church."

Dale shook his head. "I'm not into church."

Rusty slapped him on the back. "I read that *Fortune* magazine article and it said you're a man of your word."

"A man's not worth much without it."

"That's true." Rusty gave him a serious nod.

"Says so right in God's word—let your yeses and nos stand firm."

That wasn't what Dale meant but he kept walking down the line of old photos with Rusty. Julian might be worth millions, but his word was a flimsy thing. Would God prove to be different?

"Who's that?" Dale pointed.

"That's Lucy Shaw. Ezra's daughter. He tried to force that pretty thing to marry a man not of her choosing."

Evidently the Shaw patriarchs had a history of trying to marry off their daughters. "She's the one who went over the bridge."

Rusty gave him a surprised look. "You've learned a little about our history."

It felt like Dale's history, too, and in a way it was. Silas Massey was where he'd come from. Jasper Gulch held his roots. Something he'd never had or thought about before while bounced between prep school and his parents' condos.

Dale shrugged. "Faith told me about it."

Rusty gave him a serious nod. "Miss Faith's the kind of woman who'd help a man find answers to life's questions. I'd have up and married her myself if I were few years younger."

Dale laughed. "A few?"

Rusty grinned as if he knew he talked foolishness. "Quite a few."

Faith had mentioned rumors after she'd bid on

the pastor's picnic basket. Dale could only imagine what might be said about the two of them. He certainly wasn't adding more fodder to the gossip mill by discussing Faith with this guy.

"Why do you think that bridge closed?"

Rusty gave him a hard look. "The bridge remained open, but folks stopped using it. Jasper Gulch can't raise the money to fix it, either."

All information confirmed by the reports Cord had given him. "A second road in would help this town grow."

Rusty kicked the heel of his boot against the floor. "Reason enough for some to want it torn down. Folks don't like the idea of their way of life threatened by change. We're a town that holds by family values."

Dale nodded. He knew that, after talking with Cord. "What side do you fall on?"

"I've seen a lot of comings and goings in this town, but whatever will be, that's up to God."

"God?" Dale wasn't sure why the Almighty would care about a bridge in a rinky-dink Montana town.

"He's got a way of providing at the right time, so long as we trust Him. Folks round here tend to do that."

"I see." But he didn't. Not really.

As he'd told Faith, it wasn't that Dale didn't believe in God. He'd never given the topic much thought. He believed in the golden rule of treating others with honesty and respect because it made good business sense. He also made sure Massey International gave to charities because he wanted the right reputation, in addition to the tax benefits.

Faith talked freely about God. He'd once thought the way she bandied about scripture was sort of cute, but he knew better now. She lived by what she'd read within the pages of the Bible. He'd been drawn by them, too. He'd read a few passages again this morning.

The Shaw family might not be perfect, but their beliefs were a part of who they were. Belief in God seemed like part of Jasper Gulch, too. Right along with apple pie and hometown pride.

"God provides the right people."

Dale laughed. He couldn't help it. Did this old-timer think God had brought him here? Dale's presence had more to do with Julian's busy schedule than divine providence.

"Hey." Faith approached them with an attractive, scholarly looking blonde woman.

"You'll see." Rusty gave him a satisfied nod before turning his attention to the women. "Howdy, Miss Faith. Miss Robin."

"Have you been filling Dale in on his family history?" Faith asked, and then glanced at him. No doubt she wanted to know the truth, too.

"A man's got a right to his roots." The old-timer grinned with a glint of his gold tooth. "And a lot of roots have started right here in Jasper Gulch. We could use more good ones, too. You kids be good, I've got a few words for our senator over there."

Dale watched the old man leave. Dale had roots here. A history. Could he have a future, too?

"Dale, this is Robin Frazier. She's been working on her master's thesis as well as putting together a lot of these photos with Olivia Franklin, our new curator of the historical museum."

"Soon to open." Robin extended her hand. "Nice to finally meet a Massey. There's so little written about where Silas came from, only that he was a gold miner. Can you shed any light on his ancestry?"

"I did a little research online and there's no mention of where Silas came from other than Jasper Gulch. Until he skipped town." Dale glanced at Faith.

"What I've read stated his leaving caused quite a stir." Robin gave him a studious smile.

"I imagine so. Are some of those articles represented here?"

"No. Most are with the files stored at town hall until the museum opens. I'm sure Liv wouldn't mind if you reviewed them."

"Great. I'll check into that."

The woman named Robin gave him a polite nod. "Nice to meet you, Dale."

"You, too."

After she walked away, Dale glanced down at Faith. "You look puzzled."

"Surprised." She smiled, but her brow furrowed. "At what?"

She shrugged. "Your interest in Jasper Gulch's history goes beyond your great-great-grandfather."

"I needed to know the truth about Silas in order to make it right. And now I do. What your father said is true."

Her pretty mouth dropped open and then closed into a firm line. Her blue eyes caught fire. "It's not up to you to pay penance for the past. That sounds too much like my father talking."

She was pretty riled up.

"He's got a point, though. The Masseys owe something to this town."

"You don't owe anything to anyone here."

"Maybe, maybe not." Dale wanted to give back something, starting with that bridge. He pulled Faith's arm through his. "Walk with me and explain all these old photos."

The puzzled expression returned. "Sure, Dale. If that's what you want."

"It's what I want."

For starters. For now.

Chapter Twelve

Faith didn't understand Dale's sudden interest in Jasper Gulch history. Or his belief that he somehow owed the town for something his great-great-grandfather did aeons ago. This Dale Massey, who had at first appeared so arrogant and indifferent, was definitely a man of principle.

She nibbled a piece of cheese and watched Dale converse with ease. Her father had whisked him away toward the state senator and other dignitaries. Dale Massey was one refined businessman who could talk to anyone. And he was shrewd, too. Dale listened far more than he spoke.

Faith couldn't help wondering what Dale's brothers were like. Would they really come for Thanksgiving? If so, what would they think of Dale's sudden benevolence toward Jasper Gulch?

She glanced at a newspaper clipping of the first lighting of a Jasper Gulch Christmas tree. Christmas was special here. The merchants and townspeople went all out with decorations and lights the day after Thanksgiving. They strung lines of greenery with big red bells across Main Street. She wished Dale could see it, but he had important business back in New York. He was leaving....

"Hi, Faith." Pastor Ethan stood next to her with a cup of punch. "According to Robin Frazier, Mr. Massey has quite an interest in the history of Jasper Gulch."

"Yes." And then it hit her. "Can I ask you something, Pastor?"

"Sure thing."

"Would you consider a Christmas theme for tomorrow night's worship service? I could play the violin and assemble a small choir to sing carols. I'll take care of everything."

Her minister narrowed his gaze. "Why so early?"

Faith came clean. "I'd like to give Dale the gift of Christmas. A real Jasper Gulch Christmas, even if it's just a taste."

Pastor Ethan looked at her closely.

Faith didn't flinch. So what if she'd shown how much she cared for Dale by such a request? Ethan Johnson had been her minister for nearly the last six months. She could trust his discretion.

"I don't see why not."

"Thank you." Faith grinned. She'd talk to the merchants next and find out if they'd be willing to put up Christmas decorations a couple of days early. Just this once.

Pastor Ethan nodded toward the podium where her father stood.

"If everyone would have a seat, we'll get started." Her father waited while the various dignitaries took seats in chairs provided on the stage. The Jasper Gulch high school cafeteria doubled as an auditorium.

Faith pulled back her chair, and half a sheet of paper fluttered to the floor. She picked it up and rolled her eyes, ready to crumple it into a ball.

"What's it say?" Dale sat down next to her.

"I thought you were supposed to be onstage."

He winked. "I'd rather sit with you."

Her heart skipped a few beats and then she shook her head. "You, sir, are a flirt."

"You're fun to flirt with." His voice had lowered to a purr.

She tipped her head and tested the waters of Dale's feelings. "Because I'm safe?"

"Because you're not." He gave her a wicked grin, setting her heart to beat even faster with hope. "Now, what's that paper say?"

Faith handed the paper to Dale. She looked around. Folks were passing the paper back and forth, murmuring. Her father was going to have a fit.

"'Everything is NOT okay in Jasper Gulch. Where is the treasure? Who doesn't want the truth to come out?'" Dale looked at her. "It's signed LS4EVER. What's that mean?"

Faith thought about Lilibeth Shoemaker and the small stack of papers in her purse. Faith had seen those papers and they truly were a college application kit, so nothing there. It wasn't Lilibeth circulating the puzzling notes. Faith had worked with the girl setting up the tables and would have noticed had she been the one.

No. Someone else was stirring up trouble. Someone who blended in and must have passed out the notes after everyone had already arrived. But who?

She shrugged.

"And what's with the treasure?" Dale looked at her when she didn't answer.

Faith shook her head. "I really don't know. I've never heard of any lost treasure before."

She peeked at her father as he grabbed one of the papers and his face paled as he read it. Then he slowly bobbed his arms and gestured for quiet, but the crowd buzzed like a hive of busy bees.

"Okay, folks, let's simmer down. This is obviously someone's idea of a sick joke and not even worth the cheap paper it's printed on." Her father's face had reddened.

Faith read the note again. Treasure? Since when did Jasper Gulch have any treasure? Back in the day maybe…

Her stomach plummeted.

Could the note be referring to gold?

* * *

Dale took in the gamut of reactions to the cryptic message. From indifference to outrage, the audience refused to settle.

"It's about that Beaver Creek Bridge. Maybe Lucy was murdered there," someone shouted from the crowd.

"Folks, now, come on. We all know that was a long time ago." The mayor gestured for the crowd to calm down.

"What truth?" another yelled.

"What treasure?"

The townspeople were losing control fast.

Dale leaned toward Cord on his other side. As a member of the Jasper Gulch Town Council, Faith's brother had insight into all this that wasn't colored by the mayor. While meeting earlier, Cord had made no secret that he disagreed with Jackson on the bridge and other matters pertaining to the town's attempts to grow. "So what's the deal with the note?"

Cord looked frustrated and tired. "I really don't know. Ever since we started this centennial celebration back in July, there have been spurts of trouble. First, the time capsule was stolen, then some sports equipment, and then arson at the fairgrounds."

"Are they related?"

Cord shrugged and tucked one of the flyers in the pocket of his suit jacket. "Probably. But who knows? I'll make sure Deputy Calloway gets a copy of this for his file. We still don't know who caused any of it. But since that time capsule was found by the bridge, we haven't had another incident—until tonight's note."

"It sounds like you have your work cut out for you." Dale didn't envy Cord the duty of sifting through the details. Not that a poorly created note was anything illegal, but it sure stirred the pot. Did this town want that bridge opened or not?

"Welcome to small-town living." Faith gave him a sarcastic grin.

Dale smiled back.

He'd experienced some heated municipal meetings in his day and this was nothing compared to those. The people of Jasper Gulch, even when agitated, still treated each other with respect. No one hurled insults.

This place had something special, and Dale hated to see that lost with growth that wasn't managed well. He rubbed his chin. Management would be the key to the town's success.

But who'd see to that proper management?

"Morning, Mom." Faith refilled her travel mug with coffee.

"Where are you headed so early?" Her mother and father lingered at the table reading different sections of the newspaper. Ranger lay in his bed with his chin resting on a toy stuffed sheep.

Her father looked worn.

"You guys okay?"

Her mother smiled too brightly. "Fine. Why wouldn't we be?"

After last night's debacle with the note in front of a state senator from Bozeman and other county dignitaries, Faith thought her question pretty obvious.

She grabbed a muffin and wrapped it in a napkin. If her parents didn't want to talk about it, then neither would she. "No reason, I guess."

"No breakfast?" Her mom sounded disappointed, as if she wanted the added company. No doubt her mom had hoped for a buffer against the surliness of her father.

"I need to talk to a couple of store owners who didn't go last night. The Middletons, for one. I'll be back later to cut some greens."

"First Dale, now you." Her mom tried to pout. Nadine Shaw wasn't used to pouting; she usually got her way.

Faith stopped in her tracks, and her heart froze. "What about Dale? Did he leave?"

"First thing this morning. He didn't want anything to eat, either. Is something going on between you two?"

He'd said he would stay for Thanksgiving, with his brothers, too, maybe even his father. All this trouble to get the town at least halfway decorated for Christmas was for him. Had something changed his plans?

Faith raced out of the dining room, back upstairs. She didn't bother to knock on his door, and opened it wide. She spotted his opened suitcase on the bed and nearly collapsed against the door. He hadn't left for good.

Not yet.

"Faith!"

She peeked over the railing.

Her mother stood in the living room with hands on hips. "What has gotten into you? Dale went into town. He also asked if we'd mind having his two brothers and father for Thanksgiving night. He plans to leave with them first thing Friday morning. Surely he told you."

"Oh, yeah." He had told her, but she thought...

Faith didn't know what she thought. She'd panicked, thinking that Dale had left before she could show him how she felt. Actions spoke louder than words, and she had some plans yet to pull off.

Faith climbed back down the stairs. Feeling silly for her reaction, she didn't meet her mom's eyes. What was he up to with another trip into town?

"Faith? Honey, are you okay?" Her mother touched her shoulder.

"Fine. Yes, couldn't be better." She gave her mother a hug. "I'll see you later."

"See if Marie has any more of that plaid ribbon. I bought every roll that the Middleton's grocery store had."

"Will do."

Faith smiled at the dusting of newly fallen snow. She couldn't remember when they'd had this much snow at the end of November. It was as if God had blessed this gift of an early Christmas before she'd even hatched the plan. What a perfect idea, too. If she could somehow give Dale a good memory of Christmas, something his money couldn't buy, maybe it would make a difference in his life. Maybe it could change the way he viewed relationships. And her.

That's what she hoped for. Once in town, Faith turned down River Road toward Marie's house. Passing the library, she spotted a small yellow car parked there. Dale's rental.

Of course!

Dale must have come to town for better cell-phone reception and faster internet. No mystery in that. The guy had been out of commission during the power outage, so working at the quiet library to catch up made perfect sense.

Faith parked in front of Marie Middleton's tiny house a couple of homes over. Marie's pickup truck blocked the short driveway. Faith read the new logo painted on the sides of the truck—Marie's Flowers. Her friend had hopes of one day becoming a florist. For now, she worked at her parents' grocery store and kept the cooler well stocked with floral bouquets and roses. Jasper Gulch was not without some of the finer things.

Marie's favorite saying in high school had been "Where there's a will, there's a way."

Could Dale be God's will for Faith's life? Would Dale, in turn, open his heart to God? She hoped so. There she went, hoping again. But this was different than chasing butterflies. This felt a whole lot like going after what she wanted. Knocking on the garage door, she peeked inside.

"Morning, Faith." Marie Middleton looked up from the table where she worked on small floral arrangements of red carnations and rust mums with sprigs of cedar stuck in for good holiday measure.

"That's, ah…nice." Faith didn't have the heart to say otherwise. She'd never purposely put those two colors, or even flowers, together, but then, that was Marie. Her friend had an odd sense of combinations.

"Your mom already called about the ribbon. I have tons you can take."

Faith forced a smile. She wouldn't have forgotten. "Don't you need it?"

"Nah." Marie shook her head. "I can order more if I do."

Friends since high school, they'd gone their own ways to college and after, but both had returned home to Jasper Gulch after failed attempts to make it in the big city.

"Thanks."

"Your mom also said you're trying to get the merchants to decorate early for Christmas for that Massey guy." Marie gave her a wounded look. "I didn't know you liked him."

"It happened so fast, and it's not like I had the chance. The power's been out." She would have told Marie about Dale eventually. After he'd left and Faith haunted the ice-cream aisle for solace at Middleton's grocery.

Unless she convinced Dale to stay.

Marie pinned her with a hard look. "Are you falling for this guy?"

Faith shrugged. What sense was there in admitting her feelings to anyone before telling Dale? She didn't need her friend's sympathy or advice. Not yet, anyway. "He's leaving, Marie. I wanted to give Dale a taste of a Jasper Gulch Christmas before he returned to New York."

Marie shook her head as if Faith was a lost cause. "My mom says you're wasting your time on him and you'd be better off with our pastor."

Faith rolled her eyes. Rosemary Middleton kept a finger on the gossip pulse of Jasper Gulch. Winning Pastor Ethan's picnic basket had thrown gas on that fire, but they'd never even gone out! At least being seen with Dale had extinguished those rumors. "Hey, how's your dad?"

"Good. He's on an exercise plan now. Did you know they get a person right up after a triple bypass? No slacking allowed. I've been working more at the store until he can come back."

Faith nodded as Marie handed her a cute bag with the ribbon tucked inside. "You got a bill in there?"

"Yup. At cost, too."

"Marie…"

She waved Faith's protest away with stained figures from the flower stems. "Don't worry about it. I mean, it's for your mom."

Faith smiled. They used to cashier at the Middleton's grocery store together when they were in high school. She had envied her friend's tall, dark looks. But eventually, Faith had accepted her freckles and reddish hair. Tonight at church, she might even use them to her advantage by wearing that black velvet dress from the picture Dale seemed to like.

All she had to do was get him to go to church with her.

Dale stepped into the Great Gulch Grub café. An unpleasant mouthful to say; he hoped the food would prove otherwise. He smiled when he spotted one of the waitresses hanging Christmas lights in the window. He couldn't look at a string of lights without thinking of Faith.

The young minister came in right behind him. "Morning, Dale."

Dale nodded and extended his hand. "Pastor, ah…"

The guy smiled and didn't look the least bit offended that Dale hadn't remembered his name. "Ethan Johnson. Call me Ethan. Are you alone?"

"I am. Care to join me, Ethan?" Dale wouldn't mind getting the minister's perspective on opening the bridge.

Dale had reviewed Cord's information and it didn't make any logical sense to leave the Beaver Creek Bridge useless and in disrepair.

"That'd be fine." Ethan gestured for Dale to lead.

As they made their way to a booth, several people said hello, calling them *both* by name. Dale recognized Mike, the hardware store owner, and then a couple of others he'd met briefly at last night's homecoming. A little late in the morning for strictly breakfast, but a little early for lunch, Dale was surprised by the small crowd.

These were not the polite, indifferent greetings he was used to at Massey International. The folks of Jasper Gulch didn't seem to care or know who he was other than the great-great-grandson of Silas Massey. That alone seemed reason enough for the warm welcome.

Dale had to own he liked the connection, despite what Silas had done. If everyone knew about his great-great-grandfather's theft, would they treat him differently? Payback, the mayor had called it. Dale actually agreed with Faith's father, but not by his terms.

Something had to be done about that bridge and

Dale looked forward to being part of the solution. He wanted to do it. "What's good here?" Dale grabbed a menu that had been stashed between a sugar shaker and ketchup bottle.

Ethan smiled. "Everything."

"You eat here often?"

"Every chance I get."

Dale breathed in the aroma of fried potatoes and fresh coffee. "Mind if I ask you something?"

Ethan focused right in. "Go ahead."

Dale shifted under that direct gaze that seemed to see through him. "Do you want the bridge restored and opened for traffic?"

Ethan tipped his head. "I don't believe an eighty-eight-year-old accident should dictate policy. Nor flyers distributed at a local event, but both sides have their reasons. I'll go with whatever the majority decides once the funds are raised."

"What if those funds were raised? You think the mayor would reassign the resources?"

"The town council wouldn't allow that, not if the money is earmarked for the bridge, especially Jackson's son Cord. Those two have disagreed over this project since long before I moved here."

"You didn't grow up in Jasper Gulch?"

A shadow passed over the guy's eyes, but Dale could have been mistaken. "I'm relatively new and hired in as pastor to Mountainview Church of the Savior this past June. I'm from California."

Dale nodded. That would explain the pastor's easygoing, if cleaner cut, surfer look.

"You boys know what you want?" A woman well past sixty with dyed blond hair and a pencil stuck behind her ear waited for their orders.

"Thanks, Mert, I'll take my usual." The minister tucked the menu away.

Dale ordered an omelet.

"Coffee?" Mert raised the half-empty pot in her hand.

"Please." Dale flipped over his mug. He could smell fresh coffee brewing. After the waitress had gone, he looked at Ethan. "Faith says everything here is homemade."

"Yes, I believe so." Ethan looked thoughtful. "Are you planning to attend tonight's midweek service?"

"Midweek service?" Dale drew a blank.

"An informal church service at Mountainview. It would mean a lot to Faith if you did."

How close was Faith to her minister? Remembering what Nadine had said the first day he'd arrived, Dale wondered if they'd ever gone out. "You know Faith pretty well."

Ethan stirred his coffee. "Her family attends church and she helps with the music. So, yeah, I guess I've gotten to know her well enough."

They hadn't dated then. Why did that knowledge lift his spirits? "She hasn't asked me to go."

"She will." Ethan grinned. "In fact, she's playing something special for you."

Dale chuckled. "I think she's trying to make me like Christmas. I'm not much of a churchgoer, but if Faith wants me there, I'll be there."

This time the minister pinned him with a hard stare, not nearly as protective as Cord's, but serious all the same. "Faith's a warmhearted young woman."

The food arrived, giving Dale time to think how to respond while he peppered his eggs. He knew what Ethan was trying to say without really saying it.

Dale looked up to answer, but Ethan's head was bowed. No doubt praying over his food.

After that brief silence, Ethan bit into his toast. Something about the guy resonated with Dale. They came from opposite ends of the country and probably from vastly different backgrounds, but Ethan seemed as if he'd understand. Not as a man of the cloth per se, but as a man.

Dale set down his fork. "I'm not sure I can be what Faith needs. And I know I'm not even close to what she deserves."

"And what's that?"

"A churchgoer for starters. Committed and faithful for finishers." Dale watched the minister digest that statement.

He didn't look shocked. In fact, Ethan Johnson,

though young, wasn't wet behind the ears. His eyes had the look of a life lived hard.

"What makes you think you'd be unfaithful?"

Dale snorted. "I haven't had a good example of relational longevity. Not where I come from."

"New York?" Ethan looked confused.

Dale chuckled. "No. Julian Massey—my father. He's been married several times. In and out of relationships ever since I can remember."

"And you think you're like your father, bound to repeat his mistakes."

Dale shrugged. "In some ways, no, but in other ways, yes. My dad left when I was six. I don't want to do that to Faith. I don't want to be that guy who ruins her life."

"Noble sentiments." Ethan nodded. "But have you ever considered that maybe you've got it flipped around?"

"How's that?"

"What if you're worried that Faith might leave you?"

Dale chewed his toast slowly, but it had lost all taste. Were his efforts to steer clear of serious relationships more about self-preservation? Maybe. But that didn't mean he was right for Faith. They had so little in common.

"Our earthly fathers fail, but you have a Heavenly Father who's faithful. God will never let you down, Dale." Ethan wiped his mouth with a napkin.

"I've been reading the Bible lately, but I don't know. I don't see it. Some of those guys were killed for their beliefs. Isn't that the ultimate letdown?"

Ethan nodded. "We look forward to an eternal existence. Our lives here are temporary and will fade. What we do and whether we choose to live our short lives for God will impact forever. It's the only thing we take with us."

"Our reward is on the other side?" Dale had read that.

Again Ethan nodded. "I looked up your article after meeting you at the bank. It said you're a man of your word."

"I try to be." Dale shifted, uncomfortable. Feeling exposed. In business, yes, but with women? It had always been easy to keep things casual.

"God sees what's in a man's heart. Open that up to Him, and you'll choose the right path. Faithfulness is a decision made every day."

"I'll think about that." The words rang true. Choice being the key element. He'd always been honest, but pledging a lifetime together, forever? These days, that was a stretch for most. How did a man promise something like that and then deliver?

Dale had tried to make good choices his whole life. He'd never been one for rash decisions. He took his time, checked things out and weighed the consequences versus rewards before he acted. For the most part, those decisions had served him well.

Still, many of those choices were empty because he'd kept his heart as disengaged as possible. Did he dare trust it?

Chapter Thirteen

"Everything all set for tomorrow?" Faith's mom asked Cord as he entered the equipment barn.

Her mom tied a beautifully crafted plaid bow on the wreath they'd made from greens collected in the valley. Her mother, Julie and Faith had set up a worktable and, with a fire smoldering in the woodstove, it was pretty cozy. Julie had left for home and husband, while Faith and Nadine made the finishing touches.

"We've been ready for tomorrow's parade since soon after the Old Tyme wedding. As for dinner, I've been told they're all set for that, too." Cord picked through the branches of fir, pine and cedar. "What's all this for?"

Faith smacked back his hand before he pulled apart a swag that hadn't been securely wired in the middle. "Those wreaths are for our front doors. Those are for the church. The swags go on our barns and those little bundles of pine are for the church windows around the battery candles tonight."

Cord made a face. "Little early, isn't it? First the Christmas tree, and now all this?"

"Faith wants to give Dale a real Christmas before he leaves. With all this snow, it looks right."

"And Dale's family is coming." Her brother grinned and elbowed her in the ribs. "I think someone's got herself a boyfriend."

"Ha-ha." Was it true?

"Seriously, little sister, I do believe your Mr. Massey has a crush on you."

Faith shrugged off her brother's comments, but her heart did a little dance of hope, only to slip and fall. Crushes typically faded with time. If Dale had feelings for her, why hadn't he said anything? All she had to go by were the kisses they'd shared. Not a lot of clarity there when looking for a long-term relationship.

What if she was just another fling to him, a fun way to pass the time out here? She tied a bow viciously tight. Well, okay, maybe not quite a *real fling,* but close enough.

Nadine smiled. "With more Masseys to man the float, we'll have a wonderful centennial Thanksgiving."

Cord's face grew serious. "As long as whoever is circulating those notes doesn't cause any trouble."

"Well, don't mention anything like that to your father. He'll only get upset."

"Too late, Ma. We've already discussed it. I've asked Deputy Calloway to bring an extra officer to patrol the area. We really don't want any incidents at our Thanksgiving Day parade."

"I wonder what those notes were all about. What truth will be revealed?" Faith spoke her thoughts out loud.

"Well, it's all nonsense." Her mother slammed down a lopper, startling them both.

Then she up and left. Stormed right out of the barn with Ranger prancing at her mom's heels.

Faith looked at Cord. "*What* was that?"

He shrugged. "I think everyone's ready for this centennial stuff to be over."

She looked at the clock on the wall and gasped. "I've got to drop these off at the church and check on the decorations in town."

Cord helped her put the evergreen creations in a box. "Everybody was putting up garland and hanging lights when I left. You did something there and it's pretty cool."

Faith smiled.

"You really like this guy."

She nodded. It had gone far deeper than mere *like*. "I do."

"Don't jump into anything too fast."

Faith laughed. "And the month it took for you and Katie to meet and marry wasn't fast?"

Cord gave her a sheepish smile. "She's the right one for me. Look, all I'm saying is, be careful and sure. Dale Massey isn't exactly a run-of-the-mill kind of guy. He's a multimillionaire."

"I know." Her brother had said a mouthful of truth that settled deep inside Faith's heart. Nothing she didn't already know, but hearing it said out loud made it more real. Dale Massey was a multimillionaire. A man who could have everything and anyone. Why would he want her?

She let loose a heavy sigh.

"Just leave the table and tools," Cord said. "I'll take care of it."

She leaned close and gave her brother a hug. "Thanks, you're the best."

"I know."

She laughed, and loaded the box of greens into the back of her SUV. Faith turned around as Cord opened up the barn door. "Is Dale back from town, do you know?"

Again, her brother gave her a big smile. As if maybe he knew something she didn't.

"What?"

Cord shrugged innocently. "Nothing."

Faith checked her watch. She didn't have time to pry out of him whatever it was Cord thought he knew. "Gotta go."

Dale had been in town all day. Hopefully, he'd be back in time to go to church. Her stomach tripped over and sunk. She hadn't even asked him. What if, after all this, he said no?

Wait—she had his cell-phone number from the business card he'd given her that first day. That wasn't even a week ago. Maybe she rushed this, but then time wasn't on her side here. She knew her heart. Soon, Dale would, too.

Slipping behind the wheel, she keyed in his number, hoping it'd go through.

"Dale Massey."

Faith blew out her breath. "Wow, Dale. I got through. Maybe we only drop long-distance calls out here at the ranch."

"Faith?"

"Yeah." Why did she feel like a teenager asking a boy to her first Sadie Hawkins dance?

"What's up?"

She could hear the smile in his voice. Picture it, too. "Um. I'm playing violin tonight at church and wondered if, well, if you'd like to go."

"Yes."

That was it? No persuading, no hesitation? She let loose a girlish-sounding giggle and then coughed to cover up her slip. "Well, okay. I've got some errands to run, but I'll see you back at the ranch for dinner."

"Sounds good. And Faith?"

"Yeah?"

"I look forward to it." His voice caressed her ears.

Goodness, the man knew how to charm. Was that what he was doing? Or did he really mean it? If she meant anything to him, tonight she fixed to find out.

Dale drove Faith's car into Jasper Gulch. The rest of her family had gone ahead on their own. She sat in the passenger seat draped in a long gray woolen coat and black cowboy boots. Not the everyday kind of Montana cowboy boots, but nice dressy leathers. Her hair had been swept up and she wore a little more makeup than usual.

He kept glancing at her.

"Turn right." She pointed.

He did as instructed, recognizing that Main Street was a block over.

"Another right, and there's the church."

An attractive wooden structure complete with bell tower sat back on the corner. White electric candles gleamed in the windows. It looked like an old church, built maybe even before the town had been founded. Interesting, since he would have thought most mining towns were historically rough and wild places.

He pulled into the parking lot and got out. Bells chimed.

"Are those real?"

Faith looked up. "What, the bells? No. There are

real ones up there, but they don't work, so Ethan uses the recording like our previous minister."

"Why don't you get them fixed?" So far this was the only artifice he'd encountered here.

She shrugged. "I don't know if they can be. I don't ever remember hearing the real ones used in my lifetime."

He held the door open for Faith. "Don't you think it's odd how Jasper Gulch leaves things alone that need to be fixed?"

"In a small town it all comes down to priorities and funds. Not much we can do." She grabbed her violin case from the backseat.

With the opening of a museum, a historical society wouldn't be far off from forming, too. Those organizations sometimes wielded a lot of clout. He wouldn't be surprised if someday those church bells were repaired.

"Let me carry that." He held out his hand.

Faith grinned but didn't give it up. "Not on your life."

"You can trust me." It slipped out before he thought about the ramifications of that statement. He wished he knew if that were really true.

Her gaze narrowed. "Can I?"

He understood her protectiveness over the instrument, but she meant more by that question. He couldn't reassure her. He didn't know how to earn a woman's trust. His own mother didn't trust him. Was it as simple as Ethan Johnson had said? A choice made every day? "Looks like I have my work cut out for me."

That made her mouth drop open. Perfect for kissing.

He laughed before he could do that. Now wasn't the time for kisses. "What are you going to play?"

Her eyes shone with excitement. "You'll find out soon enough."

Faith was up to something and it didn't take a rocket scientist to guess that it had everything to do with Christmas. She really was his Christmas elf, spreading holiday cheer where he thought he had none.

Cars pulled into the parking lot, and men and women waved their hellos while kids dashed inside. One kid threw a snowball, only to be scolded by his mother. Dale glanced at Faith, remembering their snowball fight and the kiss that had followed. The woman was far too easy to kiss. Would that fade with time?

Dale trailed Faith up the steps. At the top, he took a deep breath. He hadn't been in a church since the last time his father got married. And it had all been for show. Neither one had attended the ornate chapel where they'd been wed. That marriage hadn't lasted but a year.

Faith turned to him, as if sensing his hesitation. "There's nothing weird beyond these doors, I promise."

He nodded. After his lunch with Ethan, he hadn't expected anything odd. The minister had given him plenty to think about. He spotted two wreaths sporting big plaid bows hanging on the doors. Again, he looked at her.

She smiled and went inside.

He followed.

"Evening, Dale." Mike Walker, the hardware store owner, offered a hand after hanging up his coat. "If the weather holds, we'll be ice fishing up on Ennis Lake in no time. Do you like to fish?"

Dale shook it. Several others had greeted him and no one seemed surprised to see him here. "I've never ice fished before. Although, I have gone for trout in upstate New York."

Mike's eyes gleamed. "Fly?"

Dale spread his arms. "Is there anything else?"

The hardware store owner laughed. "You've come to fly-fishing paradise, did you know that?"

"I didn't." Another fine tourist draw. And one more outdoor activity to look forward to in Montana.

Money can be a waste of time.

Is that what Faith had meant? That in his all-consuming pursuit of profits for Massey International, he'd wasted some precious time missing out on things that couldn't be valued with a price tag?

Dale looked for Faith to ask her but she was gone.

Her gray wool coat hung on a hanger. He placed his coat over hers.

"We'll talk," Mike said.

Dale nodded, but the sound of Faith's violin pulled his attention. He stepped into the sanctuary and openly stared. People scooted around him because he blocked the door, but he couldn't move a muscle.

Faith stood on the platform. Wearing that black velvet dress he'd seen in the photo. She looked at him and smiled.

And his heart softened and then froze. Faith's expression rivaled the one he'd envied from that picture taken in Seattle. Only there was something far deeper in her eyes tonight.

This was a Christmas gift like no other he'd been given, and Faith offered her heart right along with it. A gift he wasn't sure he could take without breaking. Eventually. He recognized the tune of "Greensleeves" and marveled at the sound. So beautiful.

Like her. Faith Shaw had a soft beauty that stole his breath away. But even more powerful was her kindness and genuine warmth. He watched her play her violin, feeling like the only one in her audience. She played for him.

He shivered. But not from the cold.

Maybe it was Faith's reaction he feared. Once she knew him really well, would he be enough to make her happy? A woman like her deserved to be happy.

He glanced at the sprigs of pine with more plaid ribbon around those electric candles in the windows. The same ribbon he'd seen on the wreaths at Shaw Ranch. Even he knew this wasn't normal Thanksgiving decor. This was Faith's doing. All because he had reasons not to enjoy Christmas.

Until now.

Faith Elaine Shaw had given him Christmas.

A woman on the piano joined in and someone dimmed the lights. Conversation hushed as a small choir of ladies took their places onstage. People scurried to sit down. And Dale slipped into a pew behind Faith's parents. The rest of the Shaws were scattered.

Nadine turned and gave him a proud smile.

He nodded.

Ethan stepped behind a podium and looked right at him. "Good evening. We've got a gift of music tonight that'll get you in the spirit of the upcoming holidays." Then, to the rest of the congregation, he said, "If you'll open your hymnals to page three hundred, we're going to start by singing 'Joy to the World.'"

Dale stood with the rest of the audience, hymnal open, but he didn't sing. He soaked in the sounds of Faith's playing and the words of a Christmas carol he hadn't really listened to before. Never had anyone gone to this much trouble for him. He'd had his share of expensive gifts and exclusive dinner invitations, but no woman had ever given him something straight from her heart.

"'Repeat the sounding joy, repeat the sounding joy…'" the congregation sang with gusto.

Robust like the rugged mountains that surrounded them, their voices blended and rose. And Dale liked it. He liked it a lot. This must be what real church was like. Rusty had mentioned the church as the people. Dale knew what he'd meant. It wasn't about the building but what happened on the inside.

Similar to that night the Shaw family had broken into song, Dale experienced a nudge of conscience. A tug at his soul. For what, he wasn't sure. The words of the hymn expressed the wonders of God's love.

Faith's gaze found his and he didn't look away. Something sweet and promising shone from her blue eyes. Something real. But would it last? Could she be the joy he needed for that pledge of forever?

After singing more songs, the choir performed a short medley of Christmas carols accompanied by Faith on the violin. Her movements were sure and graceful as she swayed with the music she made. Too soon, it came to an end and the pastor took to the podium.

But then Faith scooted next to him in the pew, and that was nice, too. He covered her hand with his own and then inched closer and whispered, "Thank you."

"For what?" She asked innocently enough, but

knew exactly what he meant. He could see the satisfaction in her eyes.

He squeezed her hand. "Giving me Christmas."

"There's more." She threaded her fingers through his.

"Yeah?"

"After church," she whispered.

Now, *that* sounded interesting. And more than terrifying.

"Come on, let's walk." Faith flipped up the hood of her coat. The temperature had dropped some and light snow fell. It couldn't be a more perfect night to take in the Christmas decorations put up by the merchants of Jasper Gulch.

Dale tucked her arm in his. "Where to?"

"Main Street. And maybe the triple G for pie. My treat."

He smiled and looked so handsome, so completely *hers*. "Sounds good."

"What did you think of the service?" She'd watched Dale soak in Pastor Ethan's message like a sponge.

"Good. I liked it there."

"First time you've ever gone to church?"

He nodded. "Pretty much, other than weddings I've attended."

Faith smiled. And he'd been with her. She closed her eyes and leaned closer into Dale as she whispered a quick prayer for courage. She hoped this wasn't the last time Dale attended church, especially with her.

They walked a block over and Faith felt a lump form in her throat when she looked down the street. Garland covered with lights glowed from business and store windows. Even the little trees in front of city hall twinkled with tiny white lights thanks to Robin Frazier and Livvie Franklin, who'd been thrilled with her plan. "Pretty, huh?"

Dale stopped and swung her around to face him. "Why'd you do all this for me?"

Faith looked up into his soft green eyes. "I wanted to give you good feelings about Christmas. I wanted you to remember Jasper Gulch." She swallowed her fear and plunged on. "And I wanted you to remember me, too."

Dale pulled her closer. "I'm pretty sure I won't ever forget you."

"No?" She hoped that was true.

He dipped his head lower. "No."

Faith closed her eyes and tipped up her face to better meet Dale's lips. Her coat hood fell back and cold snow sprinkled her hair, her forehead and cheeks. She didn't care that someone had honked a car horn, driving by.

All that mattered was this man.

The man she loved.

Faith returned Dale's kiss with urgency, pouring

out her heart because she was too afraid to vocalize her feelings. What if she told Dale that she'd fallen in love with him? Would he stay? Or would it make the time they had left awkward and strange?

Considering her father's words that lay between them, Faith wanted Dale to make the first declaration of feelings. She needed him to utter those first few words of caring. She could only show him what was in her heart and pray that he'd feel the same.

A coward's route, maybe, but Faith didn't want her words hanging in the air all alone. She pulled back and searched his eyes, giving him a chance to say those words she longed to hear and repeat. When Dale didn't say anything, she whispered, "What was that for?"

"To thank you properly."

Faith laughed to cover her disappointment. "I'm not sure there was anything proper about that kiss."

He gently adjusted her hood, pulling it back up over her head and then tucked her arm through his. "Come on, we'd better go for that pie."

Patience. She needed to slow down and practice some patience. Give Dale a chance. They had the whole evening ahead of them.

Dale put his arm around her and snuggled her close. "So what's your favorite kind of pie?"

"This time of year?" Faith giggled at the light-hearted tone of Dale's question. "Pumpkin."

"So your taste buds follow the seasons?"

Faith grinned. "Something like that. What about you?"

"I have a feeling hometown apple will be my new favorite."

Faith looked at him. "And why's that?"

"It reminds me of Jasper Gulch." He kissed her again, short and sweet. "And you."

Her heart sang as they made their way toward the café. Lights glowed through the falling snow. Great Gulch Grub had colored lights shining from every window. Dale pushed open the door for her. When they entered, a chorus of greetings rang out.

"Merry Christmas!" Mert led the charge.

"Thanks. To you all, as well." Dale grinned.

Faith shook off her coat and hung it up on the stand by the door.

"Coffee?" Mert had a pot of steaming decaf in hand.

"Tea for me," Faith said, and looked at Dale.

"Coffee."

"This way." Faith grabbed Dale's hand and pulled him through the aisle to a back booth. A tiny Christmas tree served as their centerpiece.

Dale shook his head as he slid into the red vinyl seat opposite hers. "When did you do all this?"

"I talked to some folks the night of homecoming, and finished up the rest today."

He moved the little tree toward the window and

grabbed her hands between his. "You Shaws get things done."

"That we do."

Mert delivered their drinks and then pulled a pencil from behind her ear and an order pad from her apron pocket. "What can I get for you, Faith?"

"Pumpkin pie, please. And Dale will have apple." She looked at him. "Warm with ice cream?"

"Of course."

Mert smiled at them both. "Coming right up."

"I'm supposed to give the orders, you know." Dale let go to sip his steaming coffee.

"But Mert knows me better than you."

"I was here earlier with your pastor."

Faith nearly choked on her tea. "You were?"

"Nice guy."

"Ah, yeah." Faith sipped her tea. What had the two talked about? Had Dale sought out Pastor Ethan? What for?

She waited for him to continue, but he wasn't offering up any explanations. Dale Massey didn't offer much.

"Tell me what it's like here at Christmastime."

Faith smiled. "Well, there are even more lights, and garland is hung from wires across Main Street along with big red bells and bows, and we gather in front of city hall for the annual Christmas-tree lighting."

"I think you'd love New York at Christmas.

There's ice skating at Rockefeller Center and a huge tree-lighting there."

Faith nodded. "I've watched it on TV."

He gathered up her hands again and looked at her as if he wanted to say something.

She held her breath.

"Here you go, Granny's homemade pie." Mert held two plates overhead.

Dale let go of her hands and sat back.

The moment was gone, and Faith wasn't sure how to get it back. So she silently dug into her pie as Dale did the same with his. After a few bites, she pushed her plate aside. "Well? What do you think?"

Dale drained his cup. "It's good. You're done?"

Faith shrugged. "For now."

Dale pushed his plate aside, too, and reached for her hands.

Hope sprung inside her chest as she threaded her fingers through his.

"Faith?"

"Yes?" This was it. What she'd been waiting for.

"Come to New York with me." His eyes bore into hers.

Ready to jump on that invitation, she bit her tongue instead. She hadn't heard the words she needed. So she waited. Her beating heart skipped to a clanging thud inside her chest as the seconds ticked by like a death knell. There had to be more.

There wasn't.

Releasing her pent-up breath, Faith felt her belly twist and she asked the obvious question. "Why?"

Dale let go of her hands and leaned back. "I'm not ready to say goodbye yet."

Faith closed her eyes against the burning there. *Yet?* As if goodbye was inevitable between them. She swallowed hard and opened her eyes, feeling as if the scales of her girlish dreams had fallen away to reveal the truth of what he'd proposed. Dale hadn't asked for forever. He wanted only a little while more. She'd never really had a chance. Butterflies didn't want to be caught and neither did Dale Massey.

Turning her plate around, Faith sighed. "No. I won't go to New York with you. But thank you for asking."

He ran a hand through his hair, looking uncomfortable. "Don't you think we need more time to know if this connection between us is real?"

She laughed then. A harsh sound to her ears. She didn't need any more time to know that she loved him and was prepared to spend the rest of her life with him. "For how long? A week, a month? I can't afford the hotel room for one thing—"

"Money's not an issue."

Faith's stomach turned. Of course not. Not for him. But she'd never take his money when she had no claim to it. No pledges of forever. Accepting such an invitation wasn't right, and hearing Dale make the offer turned her blood ice cold. "I have obligations here, to my symphony for one."

"Faith—"

She cut him off real quick. "I'm an all-or-nothing girl, Dale. I won't give you everything only to end up with nothing while you figure out whether or not you want me for the long haul."

"So that's it?" Dale's chin rose. He didn't like being pressed.

"Is it?" She softened then, seeing the fear in his green eyes. He was a man who relied only on himself, and marriage required God's help and guidance. "Some things you just know."

"Faith…"

"That's exactly what it takes, Dale. Faith in something larger than yourself and your own abilities. But I understand your hesitation. Really, I do."

"So now what?" His expression was hard to read. He'd closed himself up tighter than a plastic container filled with leftovers.

"We finish our pie and go home." And she'd have a good cry.

Maybe she was a silly girl who believed true love didn't need a whole lot of time to be real. Maybe she'd never learned her lesson when it came to men. Oh, her heart had mended up just fine after Scott's betrayal, but then she'd believed in lies.

With Dale, she believed in truth. They had a very real and honest love blooming. Faith knew he was right for her and that's what made it so hard to let go. But she had to. Chasing after him to New York would never accomplish what letting go might. She'd never wanted to catch butterflies with a net. She'd always hoped they'd come to her on their own.

Dale was too afraid to reach out for forever, but she wouldn't accept anything less. Faith didn't have the power to ease Dale's fears. Only God could do that.

Until Dale opened his heart to God, there was no room in there for her.

Chapter Fourteen

Amid the flurry of activity in the high school parking lot, Dale checked his watch and then his phone for texts. Nothing. Where were they? His brothers and father were supposed to be here already. The bright sunshine had warmed the day and melted snow off rooftops. It fell in clumps along the sidewalks only to thaw and trickle away.

His heart felt stone cold.

Maybe it was better that Faith had refused to return to New York with him. If he couldn't offer her forever, what was the point of trying to milk this out any longer? He'd hurt her, but she'd get over him walking away now. If he walked out on her later, she might not.

The Shaws were busy lining up floats that had been made over from the town's Fourth of July festivities. Despite the heaviness in his heart, he'd chuckled when he first arrived. Decorated tractors pulling wagons, and trailers hooked to pickup trucks served as the Jasper Gulch *floats*. A far cry from the Macy's Thanksgiving Day parade.

Faith was busy plugging in lights, fixing hay bales and clumps of fake flowers. She'd been a trouper on their way back to Shaw Ranch last night. Even though he'd stomped on her feelings pretty good, she hadn't dissolved into a fit of tears or accused him of being a selfish cad. He deserved her refusal, but he couldn't trust his feelings after so short a time. That smacked too much of how his father did things.

Faith had been kind and caring as usual. Her smiling face over breakfast had only twisted the knife deeper because he'd noticed her puffy eyes. Knowing that Faith had cried over him wasn't easy. Knowing he might be making the biggest mistake of his life wasn't exactly a cake walk, either. But how could he be sure?

He watched as each float that had been decorated in keeping with the town's history was loaded up. The Massey float was covered with mining gear. Pickaxes and sluicing gear, things a miner would use in digging and panning for gold.

He keyed his father's cell number.

"Morning, Dale." His father sounded sleepy, even though it was nearly noon in New York. Not a good sign.

"Where are you?"

"Home." His father didn't apologize or explain

why he'd chosen not to fly to Montana. He simply didn't do it.

Dale felt the jab quick and sharp. He'd asked for only one thing—for him to come to Jasper Gulch for the parade. In, and then back out of Bozeman using the Massey corporate jet. Easy. And certainly not unreasonable considering the fair weather forecast for the next few days. But Julian never did what he didn't want to. And Dale had never been a priority in his father's life.

"What about Eric and Jordan? Are they coming?"

Julian sighed. "I don't know. I haven't talked to them."

What father didn't talk to his sons after bailing? Obviously, his half brothers fared no better in Julian's world. Dale clenched his jaw to keep from saying something he shouldn't. "Did they take the corporate jet?"

"I left word that something had come up. I'm sure they got the message and are on their way."

Dale whirled around so he could see the road, hoping for some sign of his brothers. They should have been here by now, if they'd left as planned. Had Eric decided on a wild-hair trip somewhere else instead? Without bothering to tell him? What was wrong with his family?

They were not a family, that's what was wrong. They'd never been a family. He couldn't tell his father that over the phone. Not like this, in anger. It wouldn't come out right and he'd only regret saying it.

"I've got to go. The parade starts soon."

"You're taking that silly parade a bit seriously, don't you think?"

"It's a good town with good people." Jasper Gulch celebrated its heritage and forged a legacy for the generations to come. Something different than profits and mergers but more memorable. Maybe even more important.

"I need you back at the office." Not a request.

"I'll be there tomorrow." Dale disconnected.

Tempted to throw his phone across the parking lot, he tucked it into his pocket instead. And tried for calm. He turned when Faith touched his arm.

"You look madder than a mountain adder. What's wrong?"

Always caring and thinking about others, Faith deserved the best. Could he be that for her if he tried hard enough? He shook his head. "My father's not coming. I don't know where my brothers are. They're probably a no-show, too."

Faith's eyes widened. "I'm sorry."

"I'm not surprised." Bitterness laced his voice.

Some things never changed, no matter how much a person wanted them to. He might as well throw himself in that pool, too. Dale didn't have what it took to be a family man. Look at his own family. How could he expect to behave any differently?

Faith gave his arm a squeeze. "What can I do?"

Dale shrugged. "Nothing."

"Never mind the Massey float. Ride with us. I'll have them pull it out of line." She hustled away before he could stop her. Didn't matter. Nothing mattered anymore.

He checked his phone again then texted Eric's cell. Maybe he should call his assistant and find out if she'd made other flight arrangements for his two brothers. He slipped his phone back inside his coat pocket.

It was Thanksgiving. A time for family. He was done interrupting Jeannie's personal time with stupid questions he was capable of finding answers for on his own.

He'd simply have to wait and see.

Family meant something in Jasper Gulch. These people relied on each other. Dale relied on himself and his own word. It's all he had despite the many privileges wealth had given him. Returning to that life of privilege seemed empty compared to the richness he'd found here, but what choice did he have? He belonged in New York.

Dale closed his eyes. That tug inside his heart pulled harder. Like a trout on a fly line, he felt the gentle pull in the waters of his soul. He needed more than what he had. He'd always needed more.

Faith had said God never disappoints. And Ethan Johnson believed in a Heavenly Father who remained faithful. Always. Dale wanted to believe in something more but didn't begin to know how to let go and ask.

With his eyes still closed, he uttered a simple request, "Be my Father, too, God. Please, I need one that's real and can show me the way."

He opened his eyes but remained quiet a moment longer. He didn't know what he expected to feel, but when nothing really happened, he let his shoulders slump.

He thought about the work that had gone into his family's float before he'd even arrived, and a sense of belonging hit quick and heavy. An overwhelming impression of peace filled him, too.

He jogged forward and stopped Cord from moving the float.

"Thanks, but I want to ride the Massey one. Even if I'm all there is, I'm not really alone." Dale realized God had heard his prayer. And answered it.

He really did have a Heavenly Father who cared for him. Loved him without question. Without measure. Dale didn't know how he knew that, he just did. Faith had said the same last night.

Some things you just know.

Amazing.

Faith came around from the back of that float. She stood before him and searched his eyes. "You're never alone, Dale. Not here. We'd better hurry, though. The floats are ready to go."

"In a minute." Dale took her hands in his. He wanted things to be different between them but held back. Still unsure. He was afraid of forever, but he had to tell her what had happened. He owed her that much. "I, ah, prayed just now. I wanted to know who God was, and I think He showed me."

Faith's smile was brilliant and tears gathered in her eyes. "He does that."

Dale nodded. "I'm going to find out more, you know, about God. And maybe we—"

"Dale!" Two men dressed in jeans and ski jackets, each toting backpacks, ran toward them, waving their arms.

He laughed and broke away from Faith. He grabbed each brother by the shoulders for an awkward and long-overdue embrace. "You came!"

"Of course we came." Eric, the older of the two, adjusted his overloaded backpack.

Confused, Dale asked. "Why so late?"

Eric rolled his eyes. "Problems with the jet. We had to wait it out. I tried to text you, but my battery died. Jordan wanted to call, but I thought we'd make you sweat it out." His brother looked around. "This looks like a riot. Small-town Thanksgiving and all that. Maybe we'll get real mashed potatoes instead of those whipped twice-baked things served at Dad's."

Dale nodded. Thanksgivings had always been catered evening affairs worth forgetting. This one might be worth remembering with real mashed potatoes and maybe even more.

Jordan, his younger and more serious half brother, nodded, grinning like Dale had never seen him do before. "Beats going to Dad's black-tie."

Dale laughed again. "You got that right."

Julian Massey typically hosted a party at his penthouse for a few close associates on Thanksgiving evening. A boring event Dale had never had success in skipping out on. Until this year. And this year he had brothers in Jasper Gulch to share the history of their ancestry. Brothers to share that hokey Massey float!

Eric and Jordan looked at Faith and then back at Dale.

"Well, well, who have we here?" Eric grinned at her.

Faith held out her hand. "Faith Shaw. You must be…?"

Eric swept the back of Faith's hand with a kiss. "Eric Massey, at your service."

Dale draped his arm around Faith, staking his claim even though he didn't have the courage to make her his own. "All right, all right. Enough of that. This tall skinny kid is Jordan."

"Watch it." Jordan elbowed him in the ribs and nodded toward Faith. "Watch out for this guy or he'll break your heart."

Faith smiled, but her eyes glimmered with unshed tears. "I've got to go."

Dale could have clocked his brother. "Faith—"

She had pulled away, looking everywhere but at him as she gestured for them to follow her. "Come on, guys, the parade's going to start and you've got to climb up on your float."

"We're really going to ride that?" Eric pointed and laughed.

"A lot of work went into that. You can throw your stuff in my car and then we'll climb aboard." Dale unlocked his rental with a click of his key.

What did his brothers know about anything? Maybe it was up to him to show them that he could love. That love was real. Even if it came along much too fast to make any kind of logical sense.

Some things you just know.

"Nice-looking girl, but not your usual." Jordan watched Faith walk toward the large Shaw float. Then he wiggled his eyebrows. "I guess it's no surprise you stayed."

"It's not like that." Dale didn't want Faith lumped in with other women. She was different.

Jordan laughed. "Then how is it?"

"I'm working that out." Dale didn't have a definitive answer. Maybe all he needed was a little distance back in New York to be sure. If he'd learned anything in business, it was that caution typically worked in his favor. Would it work here?

The band started playing the "Stars and Stripes Forever" and the procession of floats inched forward.

"We've got to go." He clicked the lock button on his rental keys and stuffed them in the pocket of his jeans. Then he climbed onto the float with his brothers.

It was a slow crawl toward town with the small high school band in front playing their hearts out.

"Wow, this is really cheesy." Eric gave him the once-over. "Look at you, though. You've loosened up and even ditched the tie."

Dale wore jeans and the barn jacket and boots he'd purchased from the hardware store with Faith. Against his wishes, she'd dropped off his cashmere coat to the cleaners. After ruining his suit coat and two pairs of trousers, there wasn't much left to wear. "So?"

Jordan nodded. "So I think that little redhead is turning you into a Montana man."

Dale laughed along with his brothers, marveling at their perception. Was it that obvious? Dale wasn't the same man as when he'd first arrived. He couldn't be. Not after God had showed up.

Not after Faith…

Sometimes all it takes is a little faith…

The processional turned onto the same road he'd walked with her last night gawking at the Christmas decorations she'd had a hand in getting put up early. It was so easy to be with her. Kiss her.

Dale spotted the Shaw float behind them. Faith was seated between her brothers and sister, laughing at something one of them said, but her eyes still looked glassy, as if she teetered on the edge of tears. His doing.

She caught him staring and smiled.

She was beautiful, his little Christmas elf.

"Whoa. You're falling for her!" Eric sounded amazed. "How's that even possible for Dale the Coldheart?"

Dale shrugged. Anything seemed possible here.

Eric slapped him on the back. "I think I like you now."

"You didn't before?" Dale chuckled.

"Not much." His brother looked serious for a moment and then grinned. "But that's changed. You've changed."

"Thanks, I'm feeling a whole lot of love for you, too."

He and Eric had never seen eye to eye, but then maybe his younger brother had run away from Julian's approval as much as Dale had toed the line seeking it. Both approaches had been futile as their father failed to see what was right before his own nose. Sons seeking a father's love. Plain and simple.

The parade route ran the length of Main Street to River Road and they were halfway finished.

"What's after this?" Eric asked.

"Back to the high school for the centennial Thanksgiving dinner."

"Seriously? How are they going to feed a whole town?" Jordan looked skeptical.

"They'll do it." Dale had no doubts.

Kids ran alongside their float, waving and laughing. The sun warmed Dale's shoulders. Jasper Gulch had warmed him, too, but Faith had gone even deeper. She warmed his heart. Could God help him be the kind of man she deserved?

Only time would tell.

How much time did Dale need to figure out if hometown apple pie might be his favorite for a lifetime?

Faith watched Dale with his brothers. She had a good view of them on their float. They looked like brothers, they even acted like brothers. Sort of. They didn't seem to have the same ease with each other that her brothers had. But she was glad Dale wasn't all alone on that float. He would never feel alone again now that he'd asked God to be part of his life.

She couldn't be happier, and yet she'd overheard Dale confirm his presence at his office tomorrow. Dale Massey still planned to walk out of her life.

"You okay?" Julie patted her knee.

Faith nodded, but she wanted to cry. "He's leaving."

"Have you told him how you feel?" her little sister asked.

Faith shook her head. Not with words.

"Oh, Faith, don't you think he should know?"

Faith wiped her nose with a tissue. "He knows. But it doesn't matter."

Her sister gave her an understanding smile that commiserated. Julie had been there, done that. "He doesn't deserve you."

Faith laughed even though a tear slipped down her cheek. "He's a good man, little sister. Really, he is."

Julie wrinkled her nose. "He's an idiot if he doesn't love you. Besides, he's stuffy."

She glanced at Dale waving and throwing candy to the little kids on Main Street. He didn't look stuffy today. Dale Massey was a different man than the one who'd arrived a week ago. Faith couldn't even picture him in that ugly olive suit, all business-like and, yeah, stuffy.

"Do you need me to set him straight?" Adam leaned forward.

Now she'd done it. Faith shouldn't have said a word. "Stay out of it, please."

"If he so much as—"

"Leave her alone." Cord cut him off. "I already gave Dale a good talking-to."

Faith's stomach turned over and boiled. "I didn't need any help from you to scare him. Dad probably took care of that with his bogus electronics ban when the power was out."

Cord winked. "Dad tried too hard to throw you two together."

"Exactly." Faith found it hard to believe that Cord had warned Dale away, considering the twinkle in her brother's eyes. What wasn't he telling her?

"Will you kids stop arguing and throw some candy?" Nadine gave her best queen-of-the-parade wave.

Julie gave her a quick squeeze. "It'll be okay."

"Yeah, sure." Faith knew this in her head, but her heart was another matter. It ached.

She'd only known Dale a short time. It wasn't as though he'd made any empty promises. He hadn't said anything about his feelings, and that was the trouble. Dale Massey was too afraid to feel. He'd never been afraid to kiss her, though. He'd made her feel cherished and special and even…loved.

Why wouldn't Dale let go and love her?

Faith sighed and looked around. Main Street was lined with what was left of the town not already involved in the parade. She loved it here. Where else on earth would store owners decorate early for the sake of a lonely man with bad memories of Christmas?

She thought about her corner of Shaw Ranch where she wanted to build a house and raise a family. Would she give all that up and leave to marry

Dale? She glanced at him knowing she'd follow him anywhere if he truly loved her. Her answer to his New York invitation might have been different had he said that he loved her. All he had to do was commit to forever. Something Dale had said he'd never do.

Faith bowed her head and prayed for them both. She prayed for direction, she prayed for clarity, and above all else, she prayed Dale loved her enough to do just that.

After the parade, Dale marveled at the dozens of people who poured into the high school cafeteria amid lively chatter and laughter. Unlike the homecoming event, long tables had been set up in rows with white plastic tablecloths. Small vases of flowers graced each table along with large place cards announcing the families expected to sit together. The senator had remained, joined by his family, and they'd ridden one of the floats. They were placed with the Shaw family.

Family…

Dale spotted the Massey name alongside the Shaws.

"Now what?" Eric asked.

"Sit down." Dale looked around for the posters.

"Whatcha looking for?" Rusty Zidek made his way straight for him.

"The photos of the town's history. I'd like my

brothers to see them. See for themselves where we came from."

"Packed up for the museum for whenever it opens."

Dale introduced his brothers.

Rusty shook Eric's hand, then Jordan's, and then he looked the three of them over pretty good. "Well, I'll be. Mighty good to have Masseys in Jasper Gulch again. Feels right and that's a fact."

"Thanks, Rusty." Dale couldn't quite shake that *right feeling,* either.

"You might want to get yourselves some punch while the getting's good."

Dale glanced at the tables set up in each corner with cups stacked beside huge punch bowls. A crowd had gathered at each, but the far-corner table wasn't too bad. He glanced at his brothers, who looked amused as people poured over each other to meet more Masseys. Lilibeth Shoemaker was one of the ladies in line. He hoped Eric behaved.

He chuckled at the thought, realizing he cared. He'd always cared. "You guys stay here, and I'll get the punch."

"Yeah, sure. No problem." Jordan nodded as he bent his ear to an old lady shaking his hand and thanking him for coming.

It took some time for Dale to make it through the crowd, between slaps on the back and handshakes. He glanced back at his table and spotted Faith and her family slipping into their seats. He'd grab a cup of punch for her, too.

Moving forward, he bumped into the blonde woman who'd been studying the town's history. "Hi, Robin, is it?" He tapped his chest. "Dale Massey."

She smiled. "Yes, I remember."

"Do you know where the posters from the homecoming event are stored?"

"They're boxed and sitting at city hall until the museum opens."

Dale nodded. "It'll open soon though, right?"

"It's supposed to."

"It will."

Robin smiled. "You sound pretty certain of that."

"I am." Dale puffed up his chest. "I'm your first museum patron. Haven't you been offered a job there?"

A shadow crossed the young woman's face. "Yes, but…"

Dale tipped his head. "Isn't that good news?"

"Oh, yes, of course it is. I wish the very best for the museum and Jasper Gulch." The young woman looked sad.

"But you can't stay?" Dale felt for her. He also understood. He had responsibilities in New York. But maybe he could come back….

"I—well, I was only here to complete my thesis."

Dale made it to the punch table. He ladled up five cups and offered one to Robin.

"Thank you." Her attention was caught by the pastor walking onto the stage.

Dale thought the young woman looked even more forlorn. "Everything okay?"

"Yeah, sure. Excuse me."

Dale watched the troubled young woman walk away. She'd even left her punch behind. Something was definitely not right in Robin Frazier's world. Maybe he'd tell Faith so she could reach out to her. Women were better at that kind of thing.

The mayor called the room to order. "Before I hand over the mic to Pastor Ethan for a prayer of thanksgiving, I'd like to say a few words about the blessings this centennial celebration has brought Jasper Gulch." The mayor paused for dramatic effect. A true politician.

Dale braced for what was coming. He'd asked Cord to keep it quiet. At least for a little while.

"As you know, our centennial celebrations are not only about acknowledging our past but also preparing for our future. Jasper Gulch has received an anonymous but generous donation to the bridge fund that will enable us to reopen that thoroughfare and put Jasper Gulch on the map, so to speak." The mayor paused again as a cheer went up, and gave a nod toward the senator.

Eric and Jordan looked around, as did several people. Maybe looking for him. They didn't know anything about it, and neither did Julian. They would soon enough. Dale remained by the punch table and watched Jackson Shaw. Faith's father had accepted the fate of the bridge rather well. Grudgingly, maybe, but like a true man of public office, he'd spun it to his advantage.

"Today, as we count our blessings, remember that God brings folks into our lives for reasons we don't always understand. But we're made better for it. And now Pastor Ethan will bless the food."

Dale bowed his head as Ethan prayed. Dale didn't fully understand the depth of this new kinship with God, but he had a glimpse of something better. A hope he hadn't had before. And then there was Faith. Even her name reminded Dale of the God he now knew and believed in.

Could he believe for more? With God, could he be more?

After the prayer, Dale scooped up the four cups of punch and headed for his seat while Pastor Ethan gave directions to remain seated until tables were dismissed to the food line. Amazing town. Everyone chipped in.

"For you." Dale handed Faith the plastic tumbler of citrusy punch.

She leaned close. "It was you, wasn't it?"

He knew she meant the bridge donation and nodded.

She searched his eyes. "Why?"

There were too many reasons to tell them all here. "Good business decision."

"Oh." Faith looked disappointed as she leaned back in her seat and sipped her punch.

He could see the wheels in her head turning, questioning. "Faith—"

A volunteer dismissed their table. Now wasn't the time to explain his actions.

In line, Eric pointed. "Will you look at that pile of mashed potatoes? Are they real?"

The elderly lady serving behind the glass gave his brother a wide grin. "Of course they are. Everything's real in Jasper Gulch."

Dale needed to remember that when he returned to New York.

Chapter Fifteen

Later that evening at Shaw Ranch, Faith worked with Dale on the nearly finished puzzle. A fire crackled with warmth in the hearth. Her parents and Austin lounged on the sofa watching football on TV. Dale's brothers had made plans to stay another day or two and ski at Lone Peak with Adam.

Dale's plans hadn't changed. He was leaving in the morning. Taking the corporate jet back to Massey International.

Faith glanced at the animated three and shook her head. "That's trouble brewing there."

Dale took a puzzle piece from her hand. "I need that."

And I need you. She'd almost said it aloud. Almost. Faith closed her eyes against the sting of tears. She would not cry!

"Tired?" Dale rubbed the back of her hand.

She nodded, pulling her hand away. If she pretended exhaustion, she'd get away with it. Then he wouldn't know what this was doing to her. Trying to act normal when her heart was breaking. "It's been a long day."

Dale watched her closely.

Faith looked at their Christmas tree. Maybe she'd email a picture of it to him so he'd have it as a memory. A reminder to come back to Jasper Gulch.

And her.

"I'm going to make some tea. Does anyone want anything from the kitchen?" Faith needed distance from the infuriating man next to her. Didn't he realize how hard this was on her?

"Why don't you bring back a plate of cookies for the boys?" her mom said.

"Sure." Faith made her escape.

"I'll help you." Dale followed.

Faith walked in front of Dale into the foyer. If she didn't get a handle on her feelings soon, she'd shatter into pieces and that would only make matters worse.

"Hey, wait up." Dale touched her arm. "What, are you headed to a fire?"

She pulled her arm away. "Please, don't."

"Don't what?" He stood close and yet he might as well be light-years away. Cold and distant.

She faced him. "Don't pretend everything's fine, when you're leaving tomorrow morning."

He gave her an indulgent smile as if she was all of nine years old. "You know I have to go."

She wanted to throw a nine-year-old's kind of tantrum, too, kicking and screaming. What would the urbane and controlled Dale Massey do then? Faith couldn't manage anything over the lump of emotion closing off her throat, so she nodded.

Of course she knew he had to go. But why couldn't he promise to come back?

He stepped closer and searched her eyes. She'd been mistaken. Dale wasn't cold at all. There was heat in his gaze and, like the warmth of a fire, she wanted to draw closer and snuggle into his embrace.

A stupid tear escaped and Faith dashed it away.

"I've got some deals to close and business to wrap up in New York, and then I'll call you." Dale's voice came out whisper soft.

More tears. Nice brush-off line. She'd heard it all before, hadn't every woman? "Real original, Romeo."

"What's that?" He tipped his head and looked far too amused.

"I'll call you?" Her voice sounded harsh and bitter.

She didn't want to believe everything that had passed between them had only been for fun. She'd fallen too deep. For him.

Dale nearly laughed, but knew if he did, Faith might deck him and then he'd be in big trouble with her brothers. He'd never expected his beloved to have such a snarly temper. The reality that he loved her hit him hard. He'd never expected to see things crystallize into precise clarity in a single moment. The moment she'd pulled away from him and he saw the naked hurt in her eyes.

Shame filled him for trying to wait it out and get some distance to be sure at her expense. Dale didn't need distance to know what was in his heart. But then, he'd never felt this way before, so how was he to *really* know? He figured he'd obliterate any second thoughts by returning to New York. He'd think more clearly there. Get his bearings and then return.

All that flew by the wayside looking into a pair of damp blue eyes. "I'll be back, Faith."

"Yeah?" She sniffed. "When?" She still didn't understand.

"After I put my co-op up for sale."

Her eyes widened.

He rested his hands on her hips as ideas flooded his mind and hope filled his heart. He could do this. They'd make it here in Jasper Gulch. He'd make it here where it felt like home. "Maybe I can buy that old Jenkins building. No reason why I can't be the one to spearhead Massey International's dip into Big Sky real estate from right here in Jasper Gulch."

"Really?" Her eyes grew wide.

"Really. In fact…" Dale took a deep breath and went down on one knee, capturing both her hands with his. She was an all-or-nothing girl. Well, he wanted all of her.

Forever.

And forever didn't seem so impossible looking into Faith's eyes. The stone tile floor of the Shaw's foyer felt hard and cold. Not exactly the most romantic place to do this, but once started, he had to go all the way.

And it felt right.

She was right. For him.

"I'm not leaving you, Faith. I love you and I want to marry you." He laid open his heart for her, something he'd never done before, and waited.

Seconds dragged and his conviction wavered. Maybe he'd been wrong.

"Oh, Dale…" She grabbed his shoulders and her fingers trembled. More tears spilled from her eyes. She laughed then, and pulled at him to get up off the floor. "Yes!"

He scooped her up and held her tight as she laughed and cried.

She pulled back a little. "When did you decide all this?"

Dale set her down and raked a hand through his hair. "I don't know. Just now everything sort of fell into place and I knew it was right. I'm sorry I didn't do it up with roses and the whole shebang instead of the foyer of Shaw Ranch."

She giggled. "But this is where we met."

He rubbed his nose against hers. "You wouldn't pick up my keys."

"You threw them at me!" She cupped his face with her hands and stared into his eyes. "I love you, Dale Massey. You. The man you are inside."

"I know." And then he kissed her.

This is what he'd always wanted without ever naming it. He'd feared that if he acknowledged this deepest desire, he would never be the kind of man who could claim it. Faith had brought more than Christmas into his life; she'd pulled his heart out of hiding. He'd made a choice, one he would make every day from now on, and with God, his heart would remain forever faithful to one special woman.

"Is it safe yet?"

Dale heard his brother's loud whisper.

"No, no, don't go out there." Nadine's came next.

He broke away from Faith. "I think we'd better get those cookies."

"I suppose we should." The radiant smile she gave him confirmed why he'd never get enough of her.

Faith was real right down to her woolly socks. And then she laughed and gestured for her family to come closer. "It's okay, you can come out now, the show's over."

Nadine charged and nearly knocked him down when she hugged him. "I knew you were the one for our Faith. I knew it the minute I laid eyes on you."

"Thanks." Dale shook the mayor's offered hand,

but wasn't sure about the hard look in the man's eyes. Surely, his future father-in-law didn't expect him to ask permission to wed his daughter. "Jackson?"

"Welcome to the family, son."

Family.

Dale liked the sound of that. But did the mayor welcome *him* or the Massey money? It didn't really matter. He would figure out Faith's father eventually. He'd dealt with tougher men. For now, he would take the welcome for what it was worth. What mattered was Faith's love. And God's.

After rounds of congratulations, Faith phoned her sister. He could hear her laughing in the next room. Adam and Austin had gone downstairs to ready the pool table for a game while Eric and Jordan finished their milk and homemade cookies.

"So you're moving here?" Jordan asked through a mouthful of crumbs.

"Yes." Dale stretched his arms on either side of the couch. Maybe they'd build in the spring. His life with Faith stretched before him as one exciting journey he could hardly wait to start.

"Think Julian will go for it?" Eric reached for another cookie.

"He wanted you at Lone Peak. I don't see why he won't accept me in an altered role in Jasper Gulch. You can work here, too, you know."

Eric looked thoughtful. "Maybe."

That was enough for Dale. For now.

"But you're the heir, you're Dale the Coldheart," Jordan said. "What's Dad going to do without you in New York?"

Dale laughed at the nickname. "Both of you are heirs to Massey International, and Jordan, you're ready to really get your feet wet."

His youngest brother looked skeptical. "I don't know."

Dale leaned forward. "I do. God has a plan and I finally got in on it. You both can, too...."

Dale served a bigger kingdom now. Helping Jasper Gulch grow while keeping the town true to its core values is where he could better serve as heir to the Kingdom of God.

This is where Dale belonged.

Finally, he'd found his home.

Epilogue

Faith paced the living room at Shaw Ranch. It was late. Everyone had gone to bed and she glanced at the clock. Dale's plane had been late landing in Bozeman. Snow fell outside in the darkness, but it wasn't bad driving. Dale had told her so when he'd called from town. He'd be here soon.

And they'd finalize plans for their wedding and honeymoon.

Her stomach fluttered and dipped.

Dale had called her, all right. The moment he'd landed in New York two weeks ago, he'd called their landline to set the date for a Christmas wedding. Two long weeks, Dale spent wrapping up business in New York. And in Jasper Gulch, too. He'd not only bought the Jenkins building, but he'd hired a builder to renovate the top floor into an apartment. A place for them to live after they returned from their honeymoon spent in New York and then Tahiti.

Another two weeks and she'd become Faith Massey.

New Christmas memories waited to be made and they didn't want to miss a one. She heard the sound of a car pulling close and rushed outside.

"Dale!" Faith threw herself into his open arms.

He scooped her up and held tight. "I missed you."

She breathed in his subtle cologne mixed with snow and car exhaust. He even wore his red barn coat and jeans. "Are you hungry? Mom made cookies."

"In a minute." He kissed her.

She shivered.

"Let's get inside where it's warm. I've got something for you." He smiled.

"What?"

"Inside." He nodded toward the door while he grabbed his travel bag from the backseat of the SUV he drove.

"Nice rental you've got there. No lemons left?" Faith gave him a cheeky grin.

"I bought this."

Faith ran her hand along the hood of a big and brand-new jeep. "Wow. Nice."

He grabbed her hand. "Let's go inside."

Once in the foyer, Dale dropped his bag and threw his coat on the bench there. Then he led her into the living room, beyond the fireplace and in front of their Christmas tree.

Dale knelt.

She did, too. Faith knew what he'd brought her and smiled. "No roses and the whole shebang?"

"I can't wait for all that."

"Since when have you become so impatient?"

He grinned. "Since meeting you. Now, be quiet and give me your hand."

Faith sat back on her slippered feet and gave him her *right* hand.

"The other one," he growled.

She giggled and did as he asked.

Dale pulled a little black box out of his pocket and opened it. "Marry me, Faith."

She gasped at the shimmering round diamond placed deep in a vintage platinum setting of intricate filigree. "It's gorgeous."

Dale concentrated as he slid the ring on her finger. "I thought you'd like it. It's amazing, the story behind this little ring and more."

"Little?" She held her hand out and fluttered her fingers. The diamond was huge and sparkled like mad against the glow of the Christmas-tree lights.

He took both her hands in his. "My father had old photos, newspaper clippings and this ring in his safe. He said it belonged to my great-great-grandmother. Grace Massey. I had it cleaned and appraised and it's dated around the nineteen-twenties. Silas must have given this to Grace after they'd settled in New York."

Faith's eyes burned. The ring was so beautiful. "How can I accept this? It's your family's heirloom."

"You're my family." Dale curled his hand around hers. "My father agreed it should be yours. Forever. Faith, this ring was meant for your finger. Look how perfectly it fits."

Faith grinned. "You're right. It's so mine." Then she wrinkled her nose. "Do you think it was paid for with the stolen bank money?"

"Could be. But we've evened that up."

"How'd we do that?" She knew, but wanted to hear Dale admit to it. His donation to the bridge fund had been huge. And he'd become one of many new museum patrons.

"A Shaw stole a Massey's heart." He kissed her finger, near the ring. "For keeps."

Faith wrapped her arms around Dale's neck. "That's worth more than any amount of gold a bank can hold."

He rubbed his nose against hers. "I agree."

Faith kissed him then. And she couldn't help thinking the founding fathers of Jasper Gulch might be smiling down on them right along with the women who'd loved them.

* * * * *

Dear Reader,

Thank you for picking up a copy of my book. I'm thrilled to be a part of this wonderful series. Dale and Faith were a fun couple to write, coming from such opposite places. I love Faith's spunk, not to mention that she plays a mean fiddle and honors everything about Christmas. Dale is the one who surprised me most. I had him pegged as an arrogant charmer, but soon found out it was a facade he hid behind. He had everything money could buy but lacked the one thing he wanted most—unconditional love and acceptance.

We may have everything or nothing, but God, our Heavenly Father, is the one we need to please. Only through His grace can we hope to find contentment and real acceptance. And joy that surpasses any circumstance.

Many blessings to you this holiday season of Thanksgiving into Christmas.

And may God prove to be real in your life,
Jenna

I love to hear from readers. Please visit my website at www.jennamindel.com or drop me a note c/o Love Inspired Books, 233 Broadway, Suite 1001, New York, NY 10279

Questions for Discussion

1. When Dale arrives in Montana, he's irritable and doesn't want to be there. How did he treat those waiting on him? Could he have done better? How? Can you relate to where he's coming from? Or not?

2. When Faith meets Dale, she's not the least bit intimidated by him, but then something changes when she realizes who he is. How did Faith treat him? What were her first impressions of him? Were they correct?

3. How common is it to view people by their appearance? What do we see? How different is that from what God sees?

4. Jasper Gulch is a fictional place, but like most small towns, it values its history. Why is that so important?

5. Faith is a woman of faith and pretty centered because of her beliefs. How did she demonstrate this?

6. Dale comes from an affluent background. How does he view money? Does that outlook change by the end of the book? If so, how?

7. Economic growth is more challenging than ever. How difficult is it for small towns to experience growth these days? Were the folks of Jasper Gulch going about it the right way? What could they have done differently?

8. Jackson Shaw pushed Faith toward Dale without much tact. Why was that? Was he wrong to manipulate circumstances with the power outage to throw the two together?

9. Dale feels unloved by his earthly father. How can God heal that kind of wound? What steps will Dale need to take to accept God's healing?

10. Faith's passion for music keeps her content to share her talent in a regional orchestra. Should she strive to prove herself by aiming higher in the professional arena? Why or why not?

11. Faith tried to give Dale a good memory of Christmas to compensate for so many lonely holidays he'd experienced growing up. What more could she have done? Do you think she succeeded?

12. What are some of your fondest Christmas memories? What's your favorite Christmas carol?

LARGER-PRINT BOOKS!

GET 2 FREE
LARGER-PRINT NOVELS
PLUS 2 FREE
MYSTERY GIFTS

Love Inspired.
SUSPENSE
RIVETING INSPIRATIONAL ROMANCE

Larger-print novels are now available...

YES! Please send me 2 FREE LARGER-PRINT Love Inspired® Suspense novels and my 2 FREE mystery gifts (gifts are worth about $10). After receiving them, if I don't wish to receive any more books, I can return the shipping statement marked "cancel." If I don't cancel, I will receive 4 brand-new novels every month and be billed just $5.24 per book in the U.S. or $5.74 per book in Canada. That's a savings of at least 23% off the cover price. It's quite a bargain! Shipping and handling is just 50¢ per book in the U.S. and 75¢ per book in Canada.* I understand that accepting the 2 free books and gifts places me under no obligation to buy anything. I can always return a shipment and cancel at any time. Even if I never buy another book, the two free books and gifts are mine to keep forever.

110/310 IDN F5CC

Name	(PLEASE PRINT)	
Address		Apt. #
City	State/Prov.	Zip/Postal Code

Signature (if under 18, a parent or guardian must sign)

Mail to the **Harlequin® Reader Service:**
IN U.S.A.: P.O. Box 1867, Buffalo, NY 14240-1867
IN CANADA: P.O. Box 609, Fort Erie, Ontario L2A 5X3

**Are you a current subscriber to Love Inspired Suspense books
and want to receive the larger-print edition?
Call 1-800-873-8635 or visit www.ReaderService.com.**

* Terms and prices subject to change without notice. Prices do not include applicable taxes. Sales tax applicable in N.Y. Canadian residents will be charged applicable taxes. Offer not valid in Quebec. This offer is limited to one order per household. Not valid for current subscribers to Love Inspired Suspense larger-print books. All orders subject to credit approval. Credit or debit balances in a customer's account(s) may be offset by any other outstanding balance owed by or to the customer. Please allow 4 to 6 weeks for delivery. Offer available while quantities last.

Your Privacy—The Harlequin® Reader Service is committed to protecting your privacy. Our Privacy Policy is available online at www.ReaderService.com or upon request from the Harlequin Reader Service.

We make a portion of our mailing list available to reputable third parties that offer products we believe may interest you. If you prefer that we not exchange your name with third parties, or if you wish to clarify or modify your communication preferences, please visit us at www.ReaderService.com/consumerschoice or write to us at Harlequin Reader Service Preference Service, P.O. Box 9062, Buffalo, NY 14269. Include your complete name and address.

LISLPDIR13R

ReaderService.com

Manage your account online!
- Review your order history
- Manage your payments
- Update your address

*We've designed
the Harlequin® Reader Service
website just for you.*

Enjoy all the features!
- Reader excerpts from any series
- Respond to mailings and
  special monthly offers
- Discover new series available to you
- Browse the Bonus Bucks catalog
- Share your feedback

Visit us at:
ReaderService.com